T0329211

"ALL VISIONARIES MUST DIE."

Amanda tilted her head. "Doesn't 'The Demon' ring any bells?"

Julia gasped. The Demon! Luke told them about . . . they knew *everything!*

"You *bastard!*" she shrieked.

"Julia, please," Amanda murmured. She sounded amused. "Why the fuss? We asked you to play, but you didn't want to." She paused, then nodded. "Oh . . . I get it. You have something to hide. You see things, too."

"I told you she doesn't see things," Luke growled. "Only *he* does."

"But you're *also* a liar, Luke," Amanda replied. She kept her gaze fixed on Julia.

Julia's throat tightened. In a flash, the whole scenario became perfectly clear: Luke wanted to get rid of George. *Only* George. So he'd betrayed him to these psychopaths—and lied about Julia. It was beyond sick; it was beyond depraved; it was beyond anything he'd ever done.

Luke lowered his eyes, sheepishly fingering the scar on his neck.

Rat! Julia thought disgustedly. Her body trembled. Fury burned inside her. *You rat!*

"You *are* a Visionary, Julia," Amanda announced, raising her voice. "And all Visionaries must die."

About the Author

Daniel Parker is the author of over twenty books for children and young adults. He lives in New York City with his wife, a dog, and a psychotic cat named Bootsie. He is a Leo. When he isn't writing, he is tirelessly traveling the world on a doomed mission to achieve rock-and-roll stardom. As of this date, his musical credits include the composition of bluegrass sound-track numbers for the film *The Grave* (starring a bloated Anthony Michael Hall) and a brief stint performing live rap music to baffled Filipino audiences in Hong Kong. Mr. Parker once worked in a cheese shop. He was fired.

COUNT DOWN

FEBRUARY

by
Daniel Parker

Simon & Schuster
www.SimonSays.com/countdown/

First Aladdin Paperbacks edition January 1999

Copyright © 1999 by Daniel Weiss Associates, Inc. and
Daniel Ehrenhaft
Cover art copyright © 1999 by Daniel Weiss Associates, Inc.

Produced by 17th Street Productions,
a division of Daniel Weiss Associates, Inc.

Cover design by Mike Rivilis

Aladdin Paperbacks
An imprint of Simon & Schuster
Children's Publishing Division
1230 Avenue of the Americas
New York, NY 10020

Library of Congress Cataloging-in-Publication Data
Parker, Daniel, 1970–
February / by Daniel Parker. —1st Aladdin Paperbacks ed.
p.   cm. — (Countdown ; 2)
Sequel to: January.
Summary: After everyone on Earth over twenty dies, the Visionaries, a handful of teenagers hearing voices and seeing visions, gravitate towards the Chosen One, the only hope of stopping an awakened female Demon.
ISBN 978-1-4814-2587-2
[1. Supernatural—Fiction.] I. Title. II. Series: Parker, Daniel, 1970-
Countdown ; 2.
PZ7.P2198Fg   1999
[Fic]—dc21   98-45811
CIP   AC

To Ethan and Henry

The Ancient Scroll
of the Scribes:

In the Second Lunar Cycle.
In the year 5759.
The Chosen One will suffer.
Her body will weaken. Her
mind will grow dim.
And as she suffers, the earth will
suffer with her.
Heat will scorch the East—a flaming
torch to singe the land.
Cold will freeze the West—an
icy hand to harden the waters.
The Demon bides her time in
a hidden place.
And rules from an invisible throne.
The Demon will command her servants
to lead the Seers into temptation.
To break their will, to cloud their vision,
And the servants of the Demon
will destroy the Seers

Reshape time. In their own
distress, help ends soon. A
light is a dear aura 2.20.99

The countdown has started . . .

The long sleep is over.

For three thousand years I have patiently watched and waited. The Prophecies foretold the day when the sun would reach out and touch the earth—when my slumber would end, when my ancient weapon would breathe, when my dormant glory would blaze once more upon the planet and its people.

That day has arrived.

But there can be no triumph without a battle. Every civilization tells the same story. Good requires evil; redemption requires sin. The legends are as varied as are the civilizations that spawned them—yet each contains that same nugget of truth.

So I am not alone. The Chosen One awaits me. The flare opened the inner eyes of the Visionaries, those who can join the Chosen One to prevent my reign. But in order for them to defeat me, they must first make sense of their visions.

For you see, every vision is a piece of a puzzle, a puzzle that will eventually form a picture . . . a picture that I will shatter into a billion pieces and reshape in the image of my choosing.

I am prepared. My servants knew of this day. They made the necessary preparations to confuse the Visionaries—all in anticipation of that glorious time when the countdown ends and my ancient weapon ushers in the New Era.

My servants unleashed the plague that reduced the earth's population to a scattered horde of frightened adolescents. None of these children know how or why their elders and youngers perished.

And that was only the beginning.

My servants have descended upon the chaos. They will subvert the Prophecies in order to convert the masses into unknowing slaves. They will hunt down the Visionaries, one by one, until all are dead. They will eliminate the descendants of the Scribes so that none of the Visionaries will learn of the scroll. The hidden codes shall remain hidden. Terrible calamities and natural disasters will wreak havoc upon the earth. Even the Chosen One will be helpless against me.

I *will* triumph.

PART 1:

February 2, 1999
4:30 P.M. to 5:00 P.M. Greenwich Mean Time

CHAPTER ONE

Highway Four, Northeast of Haifa,
Israel
6:45 P.M.

"Where are we going?" Josh Levy asked the driver.

There was no answer.

"Let me out."

"Shut up," came the heavily accented reply.

Original, Josh thought. These two schmucks seemed to know only four English words: *shut up* and *sit down.*

"Just be thankful you're alive," the other one muttered.

Make that nine English words.

Why should I be thankful? Josh wondered, infuriated. *Without the scroll we're all gonna die, anyway. I've been your prisoner for three days now. Three days! Seventy-two hours with Jacob and Meyer, the teenage Homer Simpsons of the Israeli army. Your combined IQ doesn't add up to my shoe size. I'd be a lot more thankful if I were dead.*

'"Be thankful."

Josh closed his eyes, spent from his silent rage. He had no energy. Everything seemed to make him tired. *Thinking* made him tired. Bouncing up and down in the backseat of this dilapidated Jeep made him tired.

5

So did being around Meyer and Jacob. God, they were idiots. Baldy and Fatso, he'd privately nicknamed them. They weren't only making him tired, they were driving him insane. And the heat.

Ever since he'd been kidnapped, a freak heat wave had swept over Israel. It was the kind of heat that made his pulse race, that made his bony chest heave— the kind of heat that kept his curly black hair soaked in a perpetual sweat. It wasn't supposed to be this hot here in the wintertime. It was unnatural. It was *more* than unnatural. So much so, in fact, that Josh knew the climate must be connected to the Prophecies. In February the changes begin, the scroll had said. As the Chosen One suffers, the earth suffers with her. The cold is colder, the heat unbearably intense. . . .

But why even think about that?

The scroll had fallen out of his hands. And what these two dolts didn't understand was that Josh *had* to recover it. He *had* to get back to Jerusalem. He *had* to find Sarah. Why wouldn't they listen to him? It was crazy! *Their* lives depended on it as much as his did! *Everybody's* lives depended on deciphering the code hidden in the scroll.

"Hey, kid," Jacob said. *Haay, keed.*

Josh groaned. More than anything, he wanted to grab Jacob's machine gun and shoot him. But he couldn't move. In addition to being utterly exhausted, frustrated, and overheated, his body still ached from yesterday's drive. He'd never been on a ride like that. Ever. Now he knew what it was like to be a pinball. For some unfathomable reason Baldy and Fatso had decided to embark on a wild journey through the

6

rocky, hole-ridden, wreckage-strewn back roads of the desert. But today they were perfectly content to drive on the highway. It was ludicrous. Nothing they did made any sense.

"Hey, kid," Jacob said again. "Hey—"

"I'm not a kid," Josh interrupted flatly. "I'm fifteen. That's only three years younger than you, Fatso."

"Stop calling me that."

Josh snorted. "Why? It fits."

"Start looking for your passport."

"My *passport?*" Josh forced himself to sit up straight. His sweat-drenched T-shirt peeled off the vinyl with a sticky pop, but he hardly noticed. "Why would I need *that?*"

Jacob didn't answer. He was cleaning the barrel of his gun with a ratty cloth, his fleshy red arms jiggling as he scrubbed. He shifted in his seat, sneering at Josh over his shoulder from the passenger seat. His thick, flat lips reminded Josh of a frog. Disgusted, Josh turned to Meyer. "Why in God's name would I need a passport?"

Meyer didn't answer. He sat stooped over the wheel. Josh resisted the urge to smack his sweaty scalp. Eighteen years old, and the poor *schlub* was losing his hair. He looked as if he might drop dead at any second.

"Well?" Josh demanded.

"Because we're going to be crossing into Lebanon soon," Meyer finally answered.

"Lebanon?" Josh cried. He began to laugh—miserably, desperately. He couldn't help himself. "And you think I need a *passport?*"

Meyer and Jacob exchanged a quick glance. Jacob stopped sneering.

"What's so funny?" Meyer demanded.

"What do you think?" Josh wiped his moist brow and leaned forward. "In case you hadn't *noticed* or anything, the world is coming to an end. People are *melting.* They're gonna *keep* melting. Do you really think that the border between Israel and Lebanon means a damn thing anymore?"

Meyer's knobby white grip tightened on the wheel. "How do you know people are going to keep melting?" he murmured after a moment.

"How do you know they *aren't?*"

"How do *you* know the status of the border?" Meyer retorted.

Josh threw his hands in the air. "Because I know a pattern when I see it!" he cried. "Because nobody's in charge. Because Jerusalem, Tel Aviv, and Haifa are practically burning to the ground." His voice cracked. "Nobody's gonna care *where* you go!"

Meyer hesitated. "You seem to know a lot, Joshua," he finally stated in a tight, controlled voice. "Now let me tell you what *I* know. I know that something terrible has happened to Israel. I know that most of my superiors are dead. But I do not know what is happening *outside* of Israel. *That* is why we are going to Lebanon. That is why you need–"

"I'm not going," Josh interrupted. "I need to get back. I told you that. So let me out."

Jacob turned and thrust the barrel of his gun over the backseat. "Shut up." He jammed a clip into the firing chamber. "Shut up or I kill you."

Oh, God. Josh could feel hysteria taking hold of him. Why were they doing this? Things had gone too far. He had to escape. Too much was at stake. He'd let himself be dragged halfway across Israel—out of fear. Sarah had been right when she used to call him a wimp. But he couldn't afford to be a wimp anymore. He had to be strong, for her sake. He just prayed she was still alive. If those girls in black robes were looking for her . . .

"I have to find my sister!" he suddenly found himself screaming. "Why didn't you take her with us? Why did you leave her in Jerusalem? Why—"

"Because she's a girl!" Meyer snapped. "Do you think it was an accident?"

Josh swallowed. *A girl?*

For a moment the only sound in the Jeep was the steady whine of the engine.

"What are you talking about?" he whispered.

"I am talking about the one *other* thing I know for certain," Meyer growled. "Girls like your sister are hunting down all the survivors like us. Now do you understand?"

"Girls like my sister?" Josh's voice was quivering. "What do you mean? That's insane."

"Is it?" Meyer hissed. "Is it insane that my best friend was shot dead while your sister was standing right next to him? She's one of them, Joshua. You know it."

"One of *who?*"

Meyer didn't answer. Instead he slowed the car and flicked on the headlights.

Josh followed Meyer's gaze, peering out onto the

dusty road. Maybe three hundred yards ahead of them was a pile of sandbags. The green canvas sacks stood brightly illuminated against the blue-black evening sky.

"What is it?" Josh asked anxiously, forgetting the conversation.

"The border isn't for another twenty kilometers," Meyer breathed, as if to himself.

Josh swallowed again. He was starting to feel panicked. Why was Meyer so nervous? Things didn't feel right. The road shouldn't have been deserted. The silence was too eerie, too unnerving. If there was a roadblock, there should have been soldiers. . . .

"We should turn around," Josh whispered.

Neither Jacob nor Meyer replied. The car slowed to a crawl.

Josh fidgeted in his seat. He glanced out the rear window—and the color instantly drained from his face.

No!

A shadow scuttled across the road into the scrub brush. A shadow? Or a figure wearing a black robe?

Those girls! They followed me! They think I have the scroll!

Josh threw open the door and flung himself out of the car, hitting the hot pavement with a smack. His palms and knees burned for the briefest instant, then he tumbled end over end onto his stomach.

"Hey!" Meyer shouted. "Where are you—"

"Get out!" Jacob shrieked. *"Ambush!"*

Josh lifted his eyes, horrified. Meyer and Jacob were leaping from the slow-moving car. They rolled once on the ground and sprinted away from the open doors. There was a blinding flash, a burst of heat—then *boom!*—a deafening explosion shattered the evening air.

Instinctively Josh threw his hands over his head. Bits of fiery debris rained down on his back. The scorching metal singed his clothes and burned his skin, but he was only dimly aware of the pain. He was far more aware of the gunshots that had started popping off in every direction. He had to get out of here.

Holding his breath, he scrambled to his feet and dashed away from the smoking wreckage of the Jeep—straight into the rocky wilderness.

Is this the coldest I've ever been? Ariel Collins asked herself.

She glanced down at the icy sludge beneath her leather boots. Before she could answer that profound question, however, she had one thing to say.

Yuck.

Her boots were totally gross. They were all muddy and full of holes. A smile broke out on her face. It was a big smile, too—mixed with exhaustion, misery, and the freakish sensation that she was standing outside herself and watching some other poor loser trudge through the woods in the middle of a snowstorm. In a way, she *was* watching someone else. She was watching her boyfriend. And Brian Landau certainly didn't qualify as a "winner." Not with his filthy blond hair plastered to the side of his face and snot dripping from his nose.

Anyway, yes. This was the coldest she'd ever been. Definitely.

It wasn't that she felt a mild chill. It wasn't a matter of being only slightly uncomfortable. No. It was the kind of cold that started at the fingertips and

13

toes, and very painfully, too—as if somebody had slammed a concrete block on each little bone about a hundred times. Her nose felt as if it were about to fall off. So did her earlobes. Gradually, however, the pain lessened; it settled into a nice, dull ache by the time it reached her sagging shoulders and hips.

Oh, yeah: She'd also lost her hat somewhere. So her normally longish, decent-looking, brownish blond hair had frozen solid. Literally. If she reached up, she could snap off a handful of it, like twigs on a rotting tree.

Hey! Maybe we can use my hair to light a fire!

She laughed out loud. Her knees wobbled, and she nearly fell on her face.

Brian grabbed her arm. "Ariel? Are you all right?"

Ariel glanced up at him. Sweet Brian, the love of her life. The boy who'd made her swoon when he'd pledged his undying affection in a drunken stupor not three weeks ago. Such broad shoulders, such beautiful blue eyes. Still ruggedly handsome even when freezing to death, even *with* the boogers. Of course she was all right. Her clothing was soaked; Trevor, her demented brother, had kicked her out of town; she hadn't eaten anything but an overripe banana and six M&M's in three days . . . and now she was probably going to die in some random forest, even though Brian was somehow convinced they were on their way to sunny California.

Of *course* she was all right.

"Ariel? You want me to carry your backpack or something?"

She shook her head. *No way.* Ever since she'd left

14

home, she'd been completely obsessed with making sure she had her possessions on her at all times. Okay, yes—it was kind of pathetic, but she couldn't help it. At this point they were all that remained of her life in Babylon. Her *normal* life, the one she had before Dad melted into a puddle of slimy black gunk right in front of her eyes.

Ariel reached up to touch the strap of her backpack. She knew the contents by heart: her favorite black jeans, a hairbrush, a bunch of M&M's (thank God there were some left in the kitchen), two pairs of American-flag underwear, and a big fat dictionary-size book called *Skin Tight: The Unauthorized History of Erotic Film.*

Her smile widened. She probably should have left *that* at home. It was just too damn funny, though. She'd found it under Dad's bed last fall. He hadn't mentioned a word when it was stolen. No wonder. It was probably the cheapest, grossest, most ridiculous thing she'd ever seen. Of course, now that he was gone, it seemed a little more touching somehow, sadder. . . .

"Are you *sure* you're all right?" Brian kept pestering.

She shrugged. "I was just thinking. It's weird how things turn out, isn't it?"

He stared blankly at her through the falling snow. "You mean about Jack and Jezebel?"

Ariel almost laughed again. Jack and Jezebel? They hadn't even crossed her mind. But it *was* kind of weird that Jack had been dissolved by the melting plague about thirty seconds after Jezebel ditched him.

"It sucks, I know," Brian murmured. "Jez is your

15

best friend. But don't worry. We're gonna get her out of Babylon, away from Trevor. We're gonna—"

"Jez *was* my best friend," Ariel interrupted. She shook her head. Something had happened to Brian since they'd left town. Something *lame*. It was as if . . . well, as if all the best parts of his personality had vanished with Jack into that black gook. Brian didn't seem to *get* anything anymore. He was about as perceptive as a can opener. Didn't he understand that Jezebel had dissed them in the harshest possible way? That she had chosen to become some kind of love slave to Ariel's twit of a brother just so she could be inside where it was warm—even if it meant leaving Ariel to freeze outside? Didn't Brian realize that he should *hate* Jez for that?

But it wasn't only his stupidity, either. All his sweetness, his humor: All of it was gone. He was totally consumed by this deranged notion of going south to wait out the winter, then coming back to kill Trevor in the spring. It was *disturbing*.

She lowered her eyes.

Only a week ago—a mere seven days—she'd been absolutely convinced that as long as she had Brian, she could make it. What had happened, anyway? To her, to *them?* She'd promised she was going to start over. She'd promised she was going to be a better person. She'd promised she was going to stay by Brian's side at any cost, to go south with him, to try to salvage what they could of their lives.

Only right now, standing in the snow in the middle of nowhere . . . right now those promises seemed very, very empty.

"We gotta keep moving," Brian said.

Ariel nodded. She glanced behind them at their footprints, slowly fading in the steady downpour of white flakes. For a brief moment she had a wild flash of trying to follow the footsteps back to Babylon—back to the mob of kids hanging around the bonfire outside her house.

Forget it.

The tracks grew fainter and fainter. It was useless. She'd only end up getting *more* lost if she tried to go home. Besides, she had no idea if that bonfire was even burning anymore. For all she knew, the kids had either moved on, or were sleeping comfortably in Trevor's twisted little dormitory, or had melted away like Jack.

"Ariel!" Brian called. "Come here. Look."

Ariel turned around. *Man.* She was seriously out of it. She hadn't even noticed that Brian had gone anywhere—but he was already about a hundred feet away from her, pointing to something in a clearing.

"Come on." He beckoned to her impatiently.

"I'm coming," she mumbled. She took a deep breath of frigid air and dizzily trotted up to his side.

"Check it out," he panted, pointing over the rise. "That must be the Snohomish."

Ariel's eyes widened.

Spread below them was a huge frozen river. Where had *that* come from? It had just popped out of nowhere: a smooth band of gray ice probably a hundred yards or more across, stretching in a graceful curve as far as she could see in either direction. So Brian was right: They *were* heading south. The Snohomish was right outside Seattle.

But if the river was in front of them, then they couldn't go forward.

Great, Ariel thought. *So we're trapped. Nice going, Bri.*

"Look!" Brian cried.

Ariel stood on her tiptoes, craning her neck to follow Brian's outstretched finger. She squinted through the snow . . . and barely, just barely, she saw the silhouettes of several heavily bundled figures creeping across the frozen surface.

"Thank *God,*" she mumbled. They *weren't* trapped. If those people could cross, so could she and Brian.

"*Hey!*" Brian shrieked. He waved his hands feverishly. "*Hey! Up here!*"

Two of the figures paused. Ariel still couldn't see their faces, but one of them raised an arm and waved back.

A few moments later a distant voice floated through the air: "*Heyyy.*"

Brian grinned excitedly. "They're friendly! Maybe they have some food. Maybe we can light a fire. If they're coming from the south, I bet they can tell us the best way to go. . . ."

Ariel rolled her eyes. Friendly? They'd only said one word. For all she and Brian knew, they could be serial killers.

". . . wonder if they're from Seattle," Brian kept jabbering. "Maybe they have news. Maybe they have some idea what's *really* going on."

"Mm-hmm," Ariel mumbled. *And maybe they'll whisk us away to never-never land. Get a grip, Brian.*

About halfway across the river the people mysteriously stopped.

There must have been about fifteen of them altogether, standing in the middle of the ice. Ariel frowned. Why had they stopped?

Then the two in front disappeared.

They simply vanished from sight—straight down, like balls through a chute.

Ariel blinked. *That can't be right,* she said to herself.

But where the people had stood, only a jagged, black hole remained.

CHAPTER THREE

**Warren,
Ohio
11:36 A.M.**

2/2/99

I have to write quickly. Luke is
asleep, and he doesn't know that I
still have the diary. He can't find out,
either—I can't make him angry. If I'm
going to keep moving, I need him to do
the things that keep us alive, like
break into gas stations and light fires
in the middle of snowstorms and scare
off anyone who bothers us.

I guess there's really no point in
thinking about the bad stuff. There's no
point in thinking too hard about much at all.

When this whole horrible nightmare
first started, when all the people
melted and the power went out in New

York, I thought I was going to die. I _wanted_ to die. But once we left the city, it was like I became a different person. I can't explain it. I just knew I had to live. The visions got stronger. And they _keep_ getting stronger. Every inch I go, I can feel it, as if the visions are pulling me somehow. So until I get to where I need to be, I won't stop.

Well, unless I'm stuck. Right now we're caught in a blizzard. I know it snows a lot in Ohio, but I've never seen anything like this—the snow is so thick, you can't even see the sky. We've been sitting around at this truck stop in some town in Ohio for two days now. But as soon as the sun comes out again, I'll be on my way. I'll see the sunset, and I'll know where to go.

It's weird. Until the snow got really bad, the days were settling into this strange pattern. Wake up, try to find food, walk down the highway, rest, walk some more, try to find something more to eat (and in Luke's case, drink), and pick a place to sleep, usually an empty car. I got used to it. We passed so many piles of empty clothes and car wrecks that I stopped noticing or caring. The piles are just clothes, not dead adults. That's what I tell myself.

I keep thinking that there must be a place where there are policemen and parents, where kids like me are in school on a Tuesday morning. But the farther we go, the less likely it seems. What happened? I still don't know. To be honest, I'm not even sure if it really is a Tuesday morning. I've been trying to keep track of the days, but I might have lost count.

It doesn't matter, though. Nothing matters but moving west. I know that I'm getting closer. Almost every night I go to sleep and dream of stabbing the Demon.

Luke doesn't want to hear about it. He thinks I'm crazy. He keeps saying that if we'd gone south, we would be fine. As if it's my fault we got stuck in this blizzard. But I'm not turning south, like he wants. I'm going to keep heading west, no matter what.

Besides, things could be much worse. The power is running here, so we have light and heat and refrigerators loaded with soda. There's tons of food, mostly chips and cupcakes and stuff like that. My teeth are probably rotting. Luke found some blankets behind the cash register and made a little bed in the middle of one of the aisles. He's spent most of the time here sleeping and complaining.

I don't know how much more I can take. His temper has gotten worse. He looks terrible, too—dirty and pale and really thin.

But the worst part, the very worst, is that he keeps pushing me to go all the way.

I don't get it. In all the time we've

gone out, that's the one thing he's always left alone. Now it's all he can think about. One minute he's calling me a lunatic, and the next he's trying to get me naked. He drinks some beer and he gets all horny and starts whispering in this really weird voice. "Come on, Jules. We might die any day. Do you want your tombstone to say: 'Here Lies Julia Morrison, The Virgin'?"

It's really scary. He tries to kiss me and I can smell the booze on his breath and it makes me want to throw up. I just tell him I'm sick. <u>He</u> thinks I'm sick. I'm having flashes of the Demon every couple of hours and all Luke wants is to get his kicks.

What if he decides he won't take no for an answer?

"Ow!" Julia whispered.

A cramp shot through her wrist. She lifted her hand and shook it a couple of times. She'd been scribbling so fast and furiously that she hadn't even noticed she was in pain. But her fingers were tingling. Her back was stiff from hunching cross-legged on the floor. She felt as if her butt were twice its normal size. Maybe she should just take a little break. . . .

"Julia?" Luke's voice drifted out from behind a row of shelves.

Uh-oh.

"What are you doing?"

"Nothing," she answered. She jammed her tattered diary and pencil deep within the inside pocket of her ratty wool coat. She should have known better than to make noise. Now he was awake. It was anybody's guess what kind of mood he'd be in.

"Come here," he commanded groggily.

"In a second." She slumped back against the shelves and sighed—then caught a quick glimpse of her ghostly reflection in the sliding glass door of a refrigerator.

My God. She really *did* look like a ghost, the way her transparent image seemed to float in front of those bottles of Orange Crush. It was frightening. And she was so skinny—much skinnier than Luke. Even in the dim yellow light she could see that her long brown curls were limp and matted. Her once vibrant dark skin had lost its glow. She was wilting. It was right there, as plain as the snow outside. She was just fading away.

Luke coughed. "I said, come *here.*"

"Sorry," she mumbled. *It's just kind of hard to move when you feel like you're eighty years old.* She pushed herself to her feet. Her bones creaked and snapped like old floorboards. What did he want, anyway? She stretched, peering out the big front window into the gray-white blanket of driving snow—

Good Lord!

Two strange faces were pressed against the glass.

"What's taking you so long?" Luke demanded.

Julia's heart broke into a wild, galloping thump. Two pockmarked, greasy-looking teenage boys stood staring back at her. Right into her eyes. Their gazes were dull and unblinking—as if the sight of Julia didn't even register. One was taller, but otherwise they looked enough alike to be brothers. The shorter one's mouth hung loose. He had blackened gums and a few yellow teeth.

"Luke," she finally gasped. "Luke, get up. We aren't alone."

Luke stumbled to his feet. "What are you talking about?"

The boys glanced at each other. The taller one said something. Then they made their way toward the door.

"Luke!" Julia cried. She backed against the shelves, knocking a bag of potato chips to the floor.

"Just chill," Luke muttered, slowly plodding toward the front of the store. "I don't see—"

The door swung open. The tiny bell on the handle tinkled lightly.

Luke stopped in his tracks.

The two boys closed the door behind them and stamped their feet, shaking the snow off their boots and jeans. Neither of them acknowledged Julia or Luke. In fact, they seemed to be acting purposely *casual*—as if they'd expected to see two strangers, as if they were a couple of normal customers who had just stopped by to get warm . . . like they might have done a thousand times in the past on any cold day.

Julia held her breath.

The boys leaned against the checkout counter and wrapped their arms around themselves. They were shivering badly. Both wore only denim jackets and baseball caps. Their clothes were soaking wet. Julia couldn't help but wince. They must have been freezing.

"Cold out there," the shorter one remarked. His teeth chattered.

Julia's eyes flashed between the boys and Luke. She bit her lip. Luke inched a little closer to them.

"Ain't seen a blizzard this bad in years," the taller one drawled. His voice was oddly squeaky and high-pitched for someone so big.

Julia nodded. She forced a strained smile. *Small talk,* she said to herself. So they were just making small talk. This wasn't so bad. Maybe they were harmless. Not like those skinheads in New York. Maybe they were just average, small-town, friendly-type folks. Hope surged through her. There were still people like that left in the world, right?

The shorter one stared down the aisle at her. "Y'all seen Rob?"

Rob? Julia shook her head.

"Where is he?" the boy asked. There was an edge to his voice.

"Uh, uh—the store, the store was . . . um, empty when we got here," she stammered.

The taller one was staring at her now, too. He finally

28

stopped shivering and grinned. "Why're you so nervous, darlin'?"

Julia swallowed, but she kept smiling.

"Nobody's here, man," Luke snapped. "What the hell do you want?"

The boys turned to him.

Don't do anything stupid, Luke, Julia pleaded silently. *Please.*

"Why are y'all so uptight?" the taller one asked playfully. "We're just talkin'."

Luke's blue eyes flashed to the cash register. A long serrated knife lay beside it—the same knife he had snatched from those skinheads back in New York. Julia started to tremble. What was Luke *thinking?*

The tall one's grin grew wider. "What're you lookin' at?" he asked.

Luke's jaw tightened. He didn't answer.

The tall boy slowly turned until his eyes came to rest on the rusty blade.

"Ohhhh," he breathed.

Julia's stomach tensed.

"So that's it," the tall boy said. "You're scared. Y'all think we was gonna try to rip you off or somethin'?" He shook his head and chuckled, then glanced back at Julia. His eyes softened. "We ain't that kind of people. We're Christians."

The shorter one laughed loudly: "Hee-hee-hee."

Julia's smile faltered. There was something harsh and off-kilter in the sound of that laugh. It dredged up a forgotten memory of *Beavis and Butt-head.*

"That's right," the short one said. "We're honest Christian folk. We love thy neighbor."

29

"Uh-huh." The tall one smirked. "The key word bein' *looove.*" Without taking his eyes from Julia, he reached behind him and picked up the knife off the counter.

"Put that down," Luke growled.

The tall one cocked his eyebrow. "Damn, son. Didn't your mama teach you any manners?" He waved the knife at Luke, almost jokingly. "What's the magic word?"

Luke shrugged. "Put that down . . . *asshole?*"

The tall boy's jaw dropped. He glanced back at the short one. They started laughing.

Oh, no. Why did Luke *always* have to pick a fight? Julia's eyes darted around the aisle for a possible escape, a possible weapon—*anything.* But it was hopeless. The only way out was through the front door. And she was surrounded by rows and rows of snack cakes and Cheez Doodles, nothing hard or sharp or dangerous. Sweat began to tickle the back of her neck.

"I'm not gonna ask you again," Luke stated.

"You're not gonna *have* to ask us," the tall one said—and before the last word was out of his mouth, he lunged across the room.

"Luke!" Julia shrieked.

But the attack was too sudden. The boy seized Luke's shoulder with one hand and sliced down at Luke's face with the other. Luke tried to jerk out of the way. The blade caught the bottom of his neck. A few drops of blood spurted from his flesh onto the dirty linoleum floor. Luke dropped to his knees, wide-eyed, clutching his throat in horror. The entire fight had lasted less than two seconds.

"Bad move," the tall boy panted.

Oh, my God. Julia clamped her hands over her mouth. *Oh, my God . . .*

Luke made a faint wheezing noise. A dark red stain trickled through his fingers.

"I said, love thy neighbor," the tall boy added. He straightened and scowled at Julia. "Y'all showin' us any love?"

Julia wanted to scream, to cry for help—but fear had robbed her of her voice. She could do nothing but stare at Luke . . . slumped there against the checkout counter, his shaky hands desperately trying to staunch the flow of blood.

"I think you need to show us some love, sister," the short one whispered. "I think—"

He broke off in midsentence. Listening.

There was a sound outside the store: the unmistakable roar of an approaching car. Julia strained her ears. *Somebody's coming! Somebody can save us!*

The boys smiled at each other.

"I bet that's Rob," the short one said. "Just in time."

A pair of headlights swerved into the parking lot, then died. With them died Julia's flicker of wild hope. It was all over. *Another* sick pervert was joining them. What was going on in the world? Had everybody turned into some kind of violent psychotic? She locked gazes with the tall boy. He was methodically wiping the bloody blade clean on his pants. Luke was fighting to sit up straight.

A car door slammed, followed by the sound of uneven footsteps crunching through the snow.

"That ain't Rob," the short one spat.

The door swung open. Once again the bell jingled softly. A thin, pale boy with bright green eyes and longish dyed blond hair limped inside. He seemed to favor his right foot. Julia stared at him, baffled. Was he a friend of theirs? Did they know him? She couldn't tell. The kid looked mean, like some kind of punk rocker or something: leather coat, black jeans, heavy black shoes. He seemed younger than the rest of them.

He brushed the snow off his jacket—then stiffened.

Julia held her breath. Nobody said a word.

The boy glanced at Luke. His brow grew furrowed.

"Nothin' to see here, buddy," the short guy said.

The boy blinked. "I'm not your buddy," he replied matter-of-factly.

"Beat it, gimp," the tall one snapped.

"Gimp?" the punk asked.

He reached into his jacket and pulled out a large pistol. Julia blinked, not trusting her eyes. For a split second she thought the gun was a toy. Then the kid pointed the barrel directly at the tall boy's head and cocked the handle: *click*.

"I'm not a gimp, either."

Julia's insides turned to ice. That was no toy. . . .

The tall boy's eyes bulged in fear.

"Don't!" Julia howled. She closed her eyes and clamped her hands over her ears. "Stop it! Just stop—"

The door slammed closed, silencing her. The bell jingled for what seemed like a long time. Julia kept her eyes shut tight.

Finally a voice sliced through the still air: "Don't *ever* call me a gimp."

She forced open her eyelids. The short boy was

gone—he must have run out the door. The punk was standing next to the tall boy. He held the gun pressed against the boy's temple. Neither of them moved, but the knife trembled in the boy's hand. It looked pathetically small and harmless compared to the gun. The tall boy didn't even seem to remember he was holding it.

Julia's head spun. *Luke!* In the confusion Luke had somehow managed to push himself to his feet. But his face was a chalky white. He still clutched his neck with both bloodstained hands.

"You two," the punk called, jerking his head toward Luke and Julia. "Get in the car."

Julia nodded. There was no point in arguing. The punk had a gun. Whoever he was, whatever he wanted, however he had shown up—none of it mattered. What mattered was that he was getting them out of *here.* The blizzard hadn't stopped his car.

And even in her panicked state she knew that a car could take them farther west. Closer to her visions.

Without another moment's hesitation she grabbed Luke's arm, rushing him out through the blizzard and into the warm cocoon of the waiting backseat.

CHAPTER
FOUR

**Snohomish,
Washington
8:49 A.M.**

Ariel gaped at the frozen river. She couldn't seem to comprehend what she'd just seen. Had those people just fallen through the ice? They couldn't have. No. She felt as if she were watching a really bad made-for-TV disaster movie. But the rest of the people on the ice began scuttling back toward the opposite bank. They looked like little insects. She heard a faint rending noise, a splash. Two more of them disappeared.

Brian seized her arm. "Come *on!*" he barked.

Ariel's face soured. "What?"

"*Now!*" He tried yanking her down the hill toward the river.

"Hey!" she protested. She wrenched free of his grasp. "What are—"

"Ariel, we gotta help those people!" he shrieked. His eyes were wide. He was waving his hands. He looked like an idiot.

"Why?" she finally asked.

"Be-be . . . because they're *dying!*" he stuttered. He glared at her—then whirled and dashed down the hill. Little clouds of snow flew from under his boots as he ran.

35

So what if they're dying? Ariel wondered angrily. She shifted on her feet. She didn't mean to be harsh or anything, but this wasn't *her* problem. *Everybody* was dying. Her dad and all his friends had melted; she and Brian had seen a bunch of *their* friends melt; for all she knew, she was going to melt, too . . . and now Brian wanted to hop into a frozen river to save some perfect strangers. It made no sense. Besides, he wasn't even a halfway decent swimmer. As a matter of fact, he sucked.

Good thinking, Bri. Ariel folded her arms across her chest. Yeah. Real A-plus material. Did he actually think for one second that she would follow him? Fat chance. Whoever those kids were, they'd gotten *themselves* into that mess. It was none of her business.

The splashing and wailing grew more violent.

Ariel squinted through the snow as Brian leaped out onto the ice. He quickly shuffled toward the hole, nearly slipping several times.

Jesus.

The kids out there were all about her age. She could plainly see some drowning while others fought to pull them out of the river. Every face was twisted with panic. Why was Brian doing this? Why was he—

Brian's blond mop fell out of sight.

Oh, crap. Ariel held her breath. A moment later a pair of flailing arms shot above the surface. But they didn't look as if they belonged to somebody doing the crawl or the breaststroke. They looked as if they belonged to somebody having a fit.

Brian was drowning.

Her *boyfriend* was drowning. . . .

The next thing she knew, she was wriggling out of her backpack and flinging it to the ground. This was just great. Now *she* had to dive into that water to save *him*. She sprinted out of the woods. A heavy fog settled over her brain. Fortunately it seemed to separate what she was thinking from what she was actually doing. Her legs burned and her lungs heaved and her feet seemed to weigh about a million pounds in the snow . . . but all she thought about was Brian. She skidded to a stop at the edge of the river.

Brian was only about twenty feet away, splashing like some windup toy gone berserk. *Not good.* Ariel stepped out onto the ice and scurried toward him. She kept her eyes pinned to the back of his bobbing head. She couldn't look at the surface.

There was a loud snapping sound.

Wait a second.

The ice was giving way beneath her.

Ariel could feel it shifting. Her pulse quickened. Okay, this was a big mistake. What was she even *thinking?* She didn't know how she planned to save Brian. She was just doing the same stupid thing *he'd* done.

"Hey!" somebody called.

Another cracking sound split the air.

Dammit. "Bri—"

Her stomach shot up to her throat. An instant later blackness closed over her head. *The cold!* Burning needles seemed to tear into every part of her flesh as she plunged through the water. . . . She kicked her feet and forced her face above the surface, fighting to ignore the pain as she gulped mouthfuls of icy air. Her body shook violently. She'd been freezing for days—but this was something altogether different, something like torture.

"Ariel!"

Brian? She sputtered and blinked. Where was he? She struggled to get her bearings, but people were splashing and yelling in every direction.

"Ariel, this way!"

She whipped her head around—and caught a glimpse of him trying to pull himself onto the jagged blue-gray rim of ice.

What the . . .

That *jerk!* He'd managed to save himself! He wasn't even in trouble!

"Come on," he grunted. "Grab the kid in front of you."

Grab the kid in front of me.

In that instant, either from outrage or cold, Ariel's mind went blank. She was in no condition to help anyone but herself. Instinct took over: an instinct that commanded her to ignore everything else and get herself onto dry land. She began pawing and kicking toward Brian, past the kids who were dying before her eyes—until her fingers slammed into something hard. Two pairs of hands roughly seized her arms. Brian and some long-haired boy were tugging her out of the water. She kicked and fought and—

And then she was out.

She gasped and lay on her back, staring up at the white sky. "Ariel?" Brian croaked. "Ariel? Are you okay?"

All she could do was stare at him, shivering. She wanted to slap him. She couldn't *believe* that she'd tried to save his sorry butt when she could have just stayed put.

Brian turned back to the river. "Oh, my God," he murmured. His eyes widened. "They're all gone!"

Ariel forced herself to sit up straight. He was right. Nobody was left in the water. Only five other kids were standing or sitting there beside Brian, including the long-haired boy who had helped pull her to safety.

"They're dead," the boy muttered.

"What were you thinking, man?" Brian choked out. "Why were you trying to cross?"

"We have to," the boy answered.

Ariel's eyes narrowed. *Have to?* Her shivering grew more intense.

"We have to get to a place near here, up north," the boy went on. He waved his arms at the other survivors. They were gazing toward the opposite bank.

All of a sudden Ariel realized that she and Brian weren't on the same side where they had started.

Her heart bounced.

My backpack!

Her eyes darted frantically across the river. Sure enough, she spotted a dark speck in a sea of white, right at the edge of the dark forest.

She gasped. Her stuff . . . there was no way she could get back to it. She'd die if she got into that water again. All she could do was sit and stare at it. She'd lost everything. *Everything!* And why? Because Brian wanted to save a bunch of—

"Why do you have to go north?" Brian pressed.

The long-haired boy shook his head. "We have to get to the Chosen One."

Ariel tore her gaze from the bag. *What* had that guy just said?

"We've all had the vision," he went on, as if he were giving some kind of perfectly reasonable explanation. "The Chosen One will be there soon. We *have* to get there. It's the only way any of us will survive."

Ariel's shivering became jerky, convulsive. *Had the vision?* Okay. This guy was obviously a couple of pancakes short of a stack. Not only had she risked her life—but she'd risked it over an escapee from the loony bin.

"We can still make it, Joe," a skinny blond girl said.

The long-haired guy nodded. He took a step toward the break in the ice.

Ariel shot a quick glance at Brian.

"You're not gonna try to swim across, are you?" Brian demanded.

The boy didn't answer.

"We don't have a choice," the skinny girl said. "We *have* to find the Chosen One." She pushed herself to her feet—then jumped back into the river with a huge splash.

"Hey!" Brian shouted. "What are you *doing?* Get out of there. . . ."

But by then the other kids had leaped back in the water as well.

Ariel stared at them in utter disbelief. They must have been tripping or something. A bunch of friends had just *died*, and—

Her shivering abruptly ceased.

She glanced down at herself. What was going on?

Her clothes were frozen solid, but her body had stopped shaking. It was amazing. She was perfectly still. In fact, she didn't even feel *cold* anymore. Her frown melted away. No, in fact a sleepy warmth was spreading deep inside her belly.

"Stop it!" Brian begged the kids. "Please!"

Ariel lifted her eyes.

They aren't gonna make it, she thought with an odd, drowsy detachment.

One by one the heads began to vanish beneath the surface—slowly and with very little struggle.

Ariel sat and watched the rippling black water for a long time.

None of the heads reappeared.

Well. *That* was over.

She turned to Brian.

Jeez. He looked absolutely stricken, shaking his head, his frozen hair dangling in front of his eyes in the falling snow. Why did he care so much that a bunch of whacked-out druggies had committed mass suicide? He hadn't even been this upset on the day he learned his entire family had melted. Sure, she felt *sorry* for those kids—but compared to everything else, it wasn't exactly the tragedy of the century. No, far more tragic was the fact that she'd lost all her stuff. All that remained of her normal life.

Okay. Brian needed help. He needed a kick in the behind. He still didn't understand that they were alone, that they had to fend for *themselves.* He needed to put things in perspective. Majorly.

"Hey, Bri?" she said after a minute.

He sniffed. "Yeah?"

"You think I'll be able to find another copy of *Skin Tight* somewhere?"

41

PART II

February 2-19

FIVE

**Route 411,
Ohio
Afternoon of February 2**

George tried his best to concentrate on the road. But it wasn't easy. The two-lane highway was so damn boring. Straight as an arrow, nothing to see but snow—and not another car in sight. The steady *flap-flap-flap* of the windshield wipers was almost putting him to sleep. And the chick and the dude in back . . . well, they were starting to make him edgy.

What was *with* them, anyway?

For one thing, they hadn't said a word. Not a single, solitary peep in an hour. Not even a "hi" or a "what's up." But what pissed him off was that they hadn't thanked him for saving their lives. It wasn't that he was looking for a huge emotional production or anything. He just expected a little token of gratitude. A little common courtesy. *"Gee, pal, thanks for scaring off those hicks."* That wasn't too much to ask, was it?

He glanced in the rearview mirror. Not only were they rude, but there was this weird tension between them, too. They were sitting as far away from each other as possible. The cramped backseat of the Corvette wasn't very big, maybe big enough for one fat person.

But they were both mushed up against opposite doors. Were they boyfriend and girlfriend or what? If they were, they sure didn't *act* like it—not that George would know from experience or anything.

Hmmm.

Maybe he had made a mistake by shoving his gun in that tall hick's face. Maybe he'd rescued the wrong people. He supposed he could always toss these two weirdos out in the snow. Or at least the guy.

George stole another glance at him. *Blecch.*

The guy's neck was pretty gnarly. The knife cut wasn't all that serious or anything, but it was deep enough to make a mess. The shirt he'd wrapped around it had already soaked through with blood. It made the guy look creepy—even more creepy than he probably normally looked. His skin was really white, and his eyes were really blue, and his jaw kept twitching. George grinned. The guy looked like a freak, now that he thought about it.

The girl, on the other hand . . . now she wasn't bad at all. Nope. She was downright hot, in fact. She looked sort of like Brandy, that R&B chick who was always on MTV—when there *was* an MTV. Same long brown curls. Same smooth skin. A little thinner, even. He could just toss the guy and keep *her* along for the ride out west. . . .

"Everything all right up there?"

George jerked slightly. The guy had finally said something. Amazing. How much time had passed? Two hours? More? He looked in the rearview mirror. The guy was glaring at him.

"Everything's fine," George said, frowning. "Why?"

"No reason." The guy's voice was flat. "Maybe you should keep your eyes on the road."

A smirk crossed George's face. So they *were* a couple. The guy had caught George sneaking peeks at his girl. And he was the jealous type. George shrugged, then turned his attention back to the snowy highway.

"Be quiet, Luke," the girl said.

"Why?" the guy spat. "I don't want to crash. I've had enough near-death experiences for one day."

She sighed. "Luke, why do—"

"So your name's Luke," George interrupted loudly. If these two wanted to fight, they would have to do it on their own time. He was in no mood for hassles. "My name is George. George Porter."

The backseat was silent.

George glanced at the girl in the mirror. She was staring out the window, looking very much as though she wished she were somewhere else. Funny. He and this girl had one thing in common. *He* didn't want to be here, either.

"What's your name?" he asked.

She returned the glance briefly. He hadn't noticed how pretty her eyes were until that moment, but they were a deep, soft, almost fudge-colored brown.

"Julia," she murmured. "Julia Morrison."

George nodded. "Julia and Luke." He took a deep breath and turned to the road again. "Pleased to meet you."

Julia didn't say anything.

"Say . . . where'd you get the wheels, George?" Luke asked in an overly friendly voice. "No offense,

47

but they look a little pricey for a kid like you."

"Stole 'em, Luke," George shot back. He met the guy's stare in the rearview mirror. "Hot-wired 'em from a dead cop in Pittsburgh. Right after I busted out of the joint. Luckily the cop left his gun in the glove compartment. That's why I'm packing a thirty-eight, in case you were wondering. See, I'm what you call a *ju-ve-nile de-lin-quent.*" He lingered on the last words.

Luke blinked.

George smiled. His green eyes were hard, threatening. "No offense taken, man," he added.

Luke's Adam's apple rose and fell under the bloody shirt. He looked just a little less sure of himself than he had a second before, a little less confident. *Good,* George thought. If this jerk wanted to play tough guy, he'd picked the wrong audience.

The highway stretched on and on, unchanging. Abandoned cars and farmhouses drifted by them every now and then, but that was it. The sky was starting to grow dark. Luke was asleep in the backseat. George could hear his steady breathing.

Julia leaned forward. "George?" she murmured.

"Yeah?"

"I just wanted to say I'm sorry. I mean, about Luke. He's been really rude. But he doesn't mean it, I swear. He's just hurt and scared. You know, we've . . . we've been through a lot." Her voice fell to such a quiet whisper, he could barely hear it. "But thanks for getting us out of that store. I mean it."

George shrugged. "Whatever," he mumbled. *He'd*

been through a lot, too. He'd practically broken his leg trying to escape from jail.

"No, really," she insisted. "You didn't have to help us. I know that."

"Why *did* you help us, George?" Luke demanded.

Beats the crap out of me, George answered silently. So Luke *wasn't* asleep. He was just putting on an act so he could listen in on the conversation. George fought the temptation to stop this car and kick Luke's butt. Why *had* he helped them?

But even as he asked himself the question once again, he knew the answer. He just didn't want to admit it. This morning . . . well, he'd had this kind of premonition, a feeling. It came right after he'd had another crazy blackout. When he'd seen that truck stop from the road, it was as if he'd known there would be trouble inside. Trouble he somehow had to stop.

Of course, that was *then*. Now he didn't feel a damn thing.

"Well?" Luke prodded.

"Dunno," George grumbled.

"You know what?" Julia piped up. "We never even asked where you were headed."

George shrugged again. "West," he said. He figured he'd leave out the part about *why* he was heading west. It was none of their business, anyway.

"West?" Julia repeated. Her voice jumped. She sounded excited. "Uh . . . where, exactly?"

George peered into the mirror. A change seemed to have come over her. She was leaning so far forward that her chin almost touched his shoulder. Her eyes were wide and eager.

"Not sure yet," he said. "Why? Where are *you* headed?"

Julia cast a furtive glance at Luke. "We're heading west, too, and I was just—"

"No, we're *not,*" Luke snapped. "We're heading south."

George didn't say anything. His eyes flashed from the mirror to the road, then back. After a brief lull the atmosphere had suddenly gotten really tense again. The girl was obviously scared about something. She kept fidgeting. Why? And Luke was majorly ticked off. His blue eyes were slits, aimed straight at the back of the girl's head. His bloody fingers tightened around the T-shirt at his neck.

"So which is it?" George asked. "West or south?"

"South," Luke stated. The word was harsh and final. "Don't pay any attention to my girlfriend. She's a mental case. She hears voices and stuff like that. She needs help."

Voices? George's eyes grew wide. He swallowed, struggling to contain his excitement. She heard voices! That was sort of the same thing as having visions, wasn't it? And she wanted to go west. Maybe she *had* to go west, the way he did. Maybe she knew something about the Demon. About the Chosen One. About why *he* was plagued with those flashes . . .

"You all right, George?" Luke asked.

"What kind of voices?" George demanded. He stared at Julia in the mirror. For a second he almost forgot that he was driving a car at sixty miles an hour through a blizzard.

"What the hell does it matter?" Luke cried. He

forced a humorless laugh. "She's going crazy. Leave her alone."

"What kind of voices?" George repeated, deliberately ignoring him.

Julia shook her head—just the merest bit. She seemed to be saying: *Not now. Don't ask me now.*

"You deaf or something, George?" Luke growled.

George rolled his eyes, turning back to the highway. *Jackass,* he thought. But he'd get to the bottom of what was going on with Julia—even if he had to deal with Luke first.

"Hey, George," Luke called a few minutes later. "Just let us off at those lights up there. You've taken us far enough."

George peered through the windshield. He was about to ask, *What lights?*—when he saw a faint, fuzzy glow ahead in the driving snowstorm.

I'll be damned.

He downshifted. The car rumbled sluggishly. There was a *bunch* of lights, as a matter of fact . . . in a low building on the left side of the road. It was kind of strange; he hadn't expected to find any more signs of civilization out here in the boondocks of Ohio. There was a lighted billboard or something, too, with a bunch of pink letters. He squinted at them until he could read what they spelled.

S-P-I-R-I-T-S

Hmmm.

Spirits meant *alcohol,* right? He grinned slightly.

"Do you think anybody's here?" Julia whispered.

"I guess we'll find out," Luke muttered.

George downshifted again as the letters drifted into clear view. The billboard stood on top of an enormous liquor store. He blinked a few times. Yup, there were people here all right. Lots of them. Dozens of shadowy figures were moving behind a bank of huge glass windows. He shook his head. It almost looked as if they were *dancing* or something. They were swaying and shaking their arms and rocking their heads back and forth.

Luke snickered from the backseat. "Looks like they're having a party."

George pulled the car to a stop about twenty feet from the liquor store's double glass doors. His mouth grew slack. He couldn't believe his eyes. They *were* having a party. There must have been thirty kids in there, swigging from all sorts of bottles and dancing wildly. . . .

Hold up a second.

They were all girls!

George kept the engine running—just to be safe, in case any of them tried to pull something. But it didn't seem as if they would. What could they do? They were *girls*. He could hear the faint thump of a bass drum over the purr of the motor.

Those girls were blasting hip-hop music, for Christ's sake. They were *raging*. He started to grin again.

"What do you think we should do?" Julia murmured.

George shrugged. "I think we should check it out."

A few of the girls noticed the car. They pressed their faces against the window and immediately started smiling, waving, beckoning to the three of them to come inside. A brunette dressed only in a tank top and jeans dashed outside in the snow. She was carrying a gallon jug of wine. She ran up to George's door and rapped on the glass.

"Hey, man!" she cried as George unrolled the window. She hopped up and down to stay warm. "Come on in!"

He hesitated, smiling at her stupidly. He couldn't help himself. Was this heaven or something? She was gorgeous. She must have been around his age: sixteen or so. Her long brown hair hung down to her waist.

"What are you waiting for?" she cried, laughing. "It's freezing! Here!" She thrust the open bottle inside the car. "Drink up!"

George took the wine. It felt as if it weighed a ton, swishing around in his lap. He laughed. This was nuts. It *must* be heaven. A liquor store full of hot chicks, ready and willing to share their stash.

He glanced over his shoulder. Luke was already pushing the front passenger seat forward and fumbling with the door handle.

"Oh, you poor thing!" the girl shrieked, staring at Luke's neck and the bloody shirt. She ran around to the other side of the car and opened the passenger door for him, lifting Luke out into the snow. "You're hurt. Let me help you inside. . . ."

The door slammed.

George's gaze shifted to Julia.

"Don't go in there," Julia murmured.

George pursed his lips. *Don't go in there?* Why the hell not? What was she so upset about, anyway? Her boyfriend had almost been *killed* this morning. They needed to forget about stuff for a while. They needed to chill. A talk about visions and voices could always wait. He cut the engine and raised the bottle to his mouth.

Ahhh.

The sickly sweet liquid began to flow down his gullet, filling his body with a forgotten warmth. As it did, he was very surprised and happy to find himself thinking: *Screw the visions. If this is as far west as I make it, I'll be just fine.*

**Seattle,
Washington
February 3–7**

February 3

So. Jumping into the Snohomish River to save Brian was not the brightest decision I've ever made in my life. In fact, I'd have to say that it scores pretty near a perfect 100 on the Retard-o-Meter.

Now I'm sick.

I'm not talking sick like Jezebel was, either. Not sniffly or mildly feverish. I'm talking major chills, hot flashes, cold sweats, the whole nine yards. The weird thing is, right after I jumped in that water, I felt fine. I felt <u>great.</u> Then I got really sleepy. Brian started slapping me around—apparently he was worried that I was getting hypothermia.

It's a disease you get from being really cold. If you get it and go to sleep, you die.

Is my life just peachy or what?

February 4

Beautiful Seattle! Home of the Psychos!

There we were, Brian and me, walking down the middle of Route 5, when suddenly . . . we saw it! There, through the snow! The Space Needle, towering high above us! Thrillsville!

I wanted to turn around. I never liked Seattle in the first place, even when there <u>was</u> electricity. But Brian was all excited. He said that in the city, we were <u>guaranteed</u> to meet some people who could tell us what was going on and why everyone was melting and what the red flash was on New Year's Eve.

Sure enough, about two seconds later

this scraggly bunch of alternative rock wanna-bes appears out of nowhere and asks if we have any food.

Food? Who did they think we were? The "Chosen One"?

But it isn't even funny. Because they _were_ looking for the Chosen One. They were heading north, just like those other kids. Brian asked who the Chosen One was. They didn't know. They just said they had to find him. Oh, yeah: They had no idea why everyone was melting, either. But they said the Chosen One would probably know.

I wonder if they've drowned in the Snohomish by now.

February 5

I feel like everybody is in on some huge inside joke that I don't get. It's like they've all seen the same movie or read the same article in the _Enquirer_ or something. I'm not used to feeling that way. Back in the day, _I_ was the one who started the inside jokes. Why is it that nobody in Babylon ever heard of this "Chosen One"?

This morning I felt even worse. (Brian started sneezing and coughing, too. But he deserves to feel like crap. If it wasn't for him, neither of us would be sick.) I was just too tired to keep walking. I mean, what's the point? Seattle is just as screwed up as Babylon is. I'm starting to think the whole entire world is covered in snow and populated by a bunch of freaks. Where are all the adults? Where are all the cops? Where is anybody who has a clue about what's going on?

But Brian kept dragging me on. We found this office building on Battery Street where all these kids are hanging out. It's kind of surreal—you walk in, and you see this huge bonfire raging in the middle of this plush red carpet, right under this sign that says Citicorp. It's totally apocalyptic, like that really bad movie with Kevin Costner, <u>Waterworld</u> or whatever. They also built a pyramid out of soup cans that's like ten feet tall. There must be a thousand cans in there: Chunky, Campbell's, all the favorites. I hate soup.

The kids are really nice. Almost <u>too</u> nice. You know the type? All smiles, all generosity, and something missing—like maybe a sense of humor. I saw this PBS special on bizarre religious cults once, and the kids sort of remind me of that. (God, I hope one of them isn't looking over my shoulder.) They're kind of like Brian, actually. Just kidding.

And guess what? They're also trying to find the Chosen One. That's what I meant when I said that everyone is in on the same inside joke. (Excuse me. My brain is a little scattered right now. I think it's the fever.)

At least the kids try to explain themselves, though. For one thing, they're _not_ on drugs. They made that very clear. They've all had "visions." I'm sitting there by the fire trying to sleep, and Brian is force-feeding me piping hot split pea soup (barf-o-licious), and these kids are rambling on about how everyone's life depends on finding the Chosen One. They say that in their visions, they see this little town somewhere up north, but they don't know where it is. They just know they have to get there.

Sounds like something straight out of The Jerry Springer Show.

Speaking of which, I'd sell my soul to be able to watch The Jerry Springer Show right now. There _has_ to be someplace left in the world that still has TV, right?

February 6

Hooray! Today I feel much better. I guess all that split pea soup worked. I'm still pissed at Brian, though. Thanks to him, I haven't been able to change my underwear in four days. Thanks to him, the "Chosen One" is probably reading my copy of Skin Tight right now and scarfing the rest of my M&M's.

But my M&M's worries are over, at least. These two guys named Jared and Caleb showed up this morning. They staggered through the door, totally wasted. It was hilarious. Both have these shaggy ponytails and these grizzly beards. Caleb was smoking a joint. Jared was drinking a forty of Hamm's beer.

All the Chosen One soup losers were like, "Oh, my God! Who are these awful people?"

Anyway, it turns out that Caleb is just as big an M&M's freak as I am. He had a major case of the munchies, so he broke open his knapsack and there was one of those party-size bags of M&M's in there. He gave me as much as I could stuff into my face. As far as I'm concerned, he's the Chosen One.

It's amazing. For the first time since I left home, I actually laughed. I actually forgot about the fact that Dad is dead, that I have no friends anymore, that I don't have a home. And all I had to do was hang out with those guys for like five minutes. All they care about is getting as messed up as possible, all the time. They're really competitive about it, too, in this very dumb sort of cute little-kid way. I think they were trying to show off for me. Actual quotes:

"Dude, if you hold that smoke in

62

your lungs for thirty seconds, I'll give you the rest of my green M&M's. They heighten sexual powers."

"Dude, remember that time I filled your garbage can full of beer and drank the whole thing? I've had _twice_ as much to drink today."

Priceless, huh? I even managed to forget about all the stuff that Brian made me lose. For a while, anyway.

Today was a _total_ blast! Well, except for the end. But screw it. I'm not going to dwell on the negatives anymore. From now on, I'm going to be Miz Positivity.

Jared and Caleb and I wandered around downtown and ended up breaking into this huge sports bar/bowling alley-type complex. They had awesome games there, like Ping-Pong and minibasketball. We did four shots of Jägermeister each at the bar, then we went upstairs and played games for the whole afternoon.

Caleb kept grabbing the little basketball and slam-dunking it, screaming things like, "Caleb Walker with the monster jaaam! Who's the man? Who's the man?" He tried to get me to play one-on-one with him, but I don't know a thing about basketball. Plus I was laughing so hard that I couldn't move.

Then he curled up on the floor and passed out.

Jared found a Magic Marker and wrote I'm a chump on his forehead. Caleb didn't even wake up. Jared and I finished his M&M's. It was the best.

When he finally did wake up, the three of us went back to the bar and ran into these two girls and this guy Caleb and Jared knew from school. Cynthia, John, and Marianne. They're totally cool. Why couldn't I have gone to a school like theirs? We played quarters for a few hours and stumbled back to the Citicorp building in the moonlight.

Then came the heinous part.

We walk in, and the place is deserted except for Brian. He's sitting by the fire, crying his eyes out, holding some kid's sweatshirt and blubbering about how all the other kids went north to find the Chosen One. Then he starts in about how he misses his mom and dad, about how he's scared he's going to melt because one of the kids melted while we were gone.

I was really embarrassed. It was like "Hey, everybody, I'd like you to meet my boyfriend, Mr. Buzzkill."

But like I said, I'm not going to dwell on the negatives. One funny thing did happen, though. Caleb felt bad for Brian, so he reached into his pocket and pulled out a ten-dollar bill. Brian flipped. He was all like, "You think money's gonna make me feel any better? What's ten bucks gonna do? Money doesn't even _mean_ anything anymore!"

Then Caleb said, "I was just thinking you could use it to wipe your nose."

**Jackson,
Ohio
February 3–7**

George didn't know what the word *hangover* meant until he woke up after that first night in the liquor store. He was lying facedown on some stinky orange wall-to-wall carpeting. His stale breath was so bad that *he* could smell it. His brain felt about three sizes too big for his head. He could hardly open his eyes, they were so swollen.

How do people cope with this?

He'd gotten drunk once or twice before, but he'd never been hungover. In a weird way, though, it wasn't *so* bad. It was sort of like an initiation. It made him feel like a man. Especially since he was surrounded by a bunch of hot girls.

He'd made friends with one of them, too—Amanda, the girl who'd given him the wine, the girl with the hair down to her waist. He couldn't remember a damn thing they'd talked about the night before, but that morning she gave him some advice that he knew he'd never forget.

"The best cure for a hangover is the hair of the dog that bit you," she said.

By noon he was already plastered.

*   *   *

It took George three days to figure out how much alcohol he could handle. He calculated it to be about a bottle and a half of wine a night. Any more than that, and he would start making an ass out of himself. He learned that it wasn't a good idea to mix different kinds of booze, either.

That lesson hit home on the fourth night in the liquor store—the night he had two bottles of Ernest and Julio Gallo burgundy and a warm glass of gin. He was dancing with Amanda in the tequila aisle. He kept trying to kiss her. He would grope at her and lean forward, but she would duck out of the way. Then she ran out the front door with Luke. She was laughing. The last thing George remembered was chasing after them and slamming into a José Cuervo display case. When he came to, he was lying alone in the bathroom—wearing a bra over his head.

Luckily nobody made a big deal out of it.

"Keep your eyes closed, George," Amanda playfully scolded in a singsong voice. "You better not open them. . . ."

George grinned. He clung to a nearly empty bottle of white wine with one hand and Amanda's soft fingers with the other. The wine sloshed in the glass as he stumbled along behind her. His right ankle was still a little sore. His Dr. Martens crunched unevenly in the snow. Limping blindly and drunkenly through the woods was *kind* of fun . . . but how much farther did they have to go? It seemed as though they'd been walking all afternoon. Up and down hills, across puddles, over at least two tree trunks—he'd nearly fallen on his face more than once.

"Almost there!" Amanda cried. "Hang on!"

Finally she stopped. She placed her hands on his shoulders and gently shifted his position.

"Ready?" she asked.

He nodded. "You bet."

"Okay. Take a peek."

George's eyelids fluttered open.

"Surprise!" a chorus of female voices sang.

Wow . . .

Every single one of the girls from the liquor store was standing on the front porch of an old-fashioned, Victorian-style mansion. All of them were raising wineglasses. They were giggling, toasting him, chattering away like a bunch of hens. . . .

George shook his head. The house was one of the most beautiful he'd ever seen—with tall bay windows, a turret on one side, and sloping snow-covered roofs. Soft lights burned behind the thick curtains. Tendrils of smoke wafted up from a high stone chimney. The girls laughed and laughed. His mind couldn't seem to process it all. It was a sensory overload. He swayed, feeling dizzy.

There was a rushing noise in his ears.

The girls' laughter grew muffled.

Oh, no, he thought. *Not now!*

"George?" Amanda asked. Her voice sounded miles away. "You all right?"

He couldn't answer. He struggled to hold on to consciousness, but the mob of girls swirled before his eyes. He pitched forward—

I'm running away from the cliff.

The Demon is behind me. I can feel its heat on the back of my neck. But I won't let go of my baby. I won't let her fall. I stare down at her, and she stares back at me. She has the most gorgeous eyes, one green and one brown. . . .

"George?"

He was lying on his back, gazing up at Amanda. Her face was creased with worry.

Oh, brother.

"Are you all right?" she asked.

He forced himself to nod. The fear was gone. Now he was just dazed and embarrassed. He figured he had two choices: Either he could play the whole thing off as if he passed out for a second, or he could admit the truth.

Yeah, right. Like he would really admit to this fine girl that he had strange "visions" of an unborn baby with messed-up eyes.

Sorry, Amanda. I should have told you earlier, but I'm a nutcase.

"I'm fine," he said, pushing himself to his feet. He brushed himself off and glanced at the wine bottle, lying beside him in the snow. "Musta had a little too much on the way over," he lied. "So are we gonna party or what?"

Another night, another blowout.

George sat on the edge of a bed in one of the mansion's many dimly lit rooms, sipping from a wineglass and watching Luke flirt with one of the girls. The steady thump of a hip-hop drum track was pounding through the walls. George had never been a huge fan of rap music before, but now . . . hell, now he could see himself getting into it. It made these girls *dance.*

A few of them were shaking their hips in the room—but Luke was just leaning by the windowsill, staring into this one girl's eyes and whispering to her. George shook his head. As much as he hated to admit it, he had to hand it to the jerk: Luke knew how to handle chicks. His girlfriend didn't even seem to care that much. At least not enough to make a big deal. Julia just spent her life sulking.

"George?"

He glanced up—and immediately straightened. *Hot damn!*

Amanda was snaking her way through the dancing girls. George swallowed and squirmed on the mattress. She was wearing really, *really* tight black vinyl pants—and one of those short-cropped T-shirts. He could see her belly button. He could see her smooth, white, flat stomach. . . .

She plopped down beside him.

"So how's it going, George?" she murmured. Without a word of warning, she casually reached over and ran her fingers through his stringy hair.

"Okay," he said. He shrugged and lowered his eyes—fighting with every ounce of his strength to act as cool as possible. Unfortunately his right leg started twitching. His blood pounded straight to his face. *Relax, goddammit!* he ordered himself. But he couldn't. Amanda kept stroking his scalp. Her fingers felt like hot little worms. He stared at his knee, bouncing up and down. So much for being suave. He looked as if he were having a freaking seizure.

". . . having fun with us?"

"Huh?" His head jerked up. His voice squeaked. He blushed again—but thankfully she just kept smiling, as if she didn't notice. "What was that?"

"I just wanted to know if you're having a good time."

He nodded spastically.

"Good," she breathed. Her fingers wandered toward his neck. "Because having a good time is important. It's all we have left."

He blinked. "Uh . . . what, um, what do you mean?"

She laughed. "Haven't you ever wondered what's happening to the world?"

"Well, uh—I mean, yeah," he stuttered. He glanced at her, then back at his wineglass. "I've wondered a lot, actually."

"So have I," she said. "But then my friends and I just kind of figured, what's the point of *wondering?* Are we even gonna figure out what happened? Are we even gonna be able to stop it? Probably not. We're all gonna end up melting, just like everyone else."

George took a sip of wine. He had no clue what to say to that. He was barely listening. All he could think about was . . . *the hand.* It kept moving lower and lower, softly brushing the nape of his neck.

"So we have a philosophy," she whispered, leaning closer. "We should all just get our kicks while we can. Don't you agree?"

He nodded again. His heart felt as if it were about to explode. He drained the rest of his glass in one gulp.

"You like what you see here, don't you?" she asked. "You like what we've done with this town. You like what we've done with this house. You like *me.*" Her dark eyes bored into George's own. "And I like you."

George swallowed. *This is it!* It was finally going to happen, wasn't it? Wasn't it? Praise the Lord! After sixteen long years he was finally going to lose his—

She abruptly withdrew her hand. "But I have to ask you something, George," she stated.

"Huh?" He stared at her, bewildered. *Oh, no.* She wasn't smiling anymore. "What is it?" he asked. His voice was thick. "What's the matter?"

"Well, to be honest, I'm a little worried about you."

"Worried about me?" he repeated uncomprehendingly. That was ridiculous. How could she be worried? She'd just said that her philosophy was not to worry about *anything.* Well, that was sort of what she'd said, anyhow.

"Yes, George," she said. "I don't know if you're altogether . . . healthy."

His face fell. "Healthy? What do you mean?"

She grinned. "I don't mean it in a bad way. It's just that yesterday, when you passed out in the snow, it reminded me of something." She sighed and leaned back on the mattress, resting on her elbows. Her curly black hair cascaded down over her shoulders. "See, there was a guy who lived in this town just before you guys showed up. He was a good friend of mine. He vaporized."

"So?" George demanded. He shook his head. *Lots* of people vaporized. *Most* people vaporized. What did that have to do with him?

"The point is—right *before* he vaporized, he started passing out all the time," she said. "He said he was having these weird visions." She paused and looked at George meaningfully. "Are *you* having weird visions, George? Do you see things?"

George chewed his lip. So *that's* what this was all about. He looked at her, then glanced into his lap, agitatedly rolling the stem of the empty wineglass in his fingers. *Shoot!* He knew those flashes were bad news. Did she think he was going to vaporize? If she did, she probably didn't want a damn thing to do with him. Obviously not. That's why she asked the question.

"It's okay if you see things," she prodded.

"But I *don't,*" he insisted. "I *swear.*"

She gazed at him for a second, then stood and patted his knee. "Okay, George," she murmured. "Okay." With that, she strode from the room.

"Hey!" George called after her. He knew he sounded desperate—but he couldn't help it. "Hey! Where are you going? Where . . . ?"

But his voice was lost in the droning music.

She was gone.

Kibbutz Yehi'am, near Nahariya,
Israel
Afternoon of February 8

By the time Josh finished packing a duffel bag with some of the nonperishable foods from the abandoned storeroom—the cereals, the soups, the dried fruits—he finally convinced himself that he was ready to head south to Jerusalem.

It had taken six whole days to work up the courage to leave the deserted kibbutz: six days of hiding out in terror. The memory of the exploding Jeep and the gunfire still haunted him every waking moment. He'd been so close to dying. Too close.

Why didn't they chase me? he wondered again. *Why?*

Maybe the black-robed girls figured he would just die. It would have been a fairly reasonable assumption. He was alone in a foreign country, temperatures had climbed well into the hundreds, and *somebody* had systematically murdered every single survivor near the Lebanese border. Nahariya, the northernmost town on the coast, had been decimated.

Everybody was dead. *Everybody.*

He shuddered.

The slaughter . . . God, it was incomprehensible. The streets of Narahiya were not only littered with the now familiar piles of clothes; they were strewn with the shot and bloodied bodies of hundreds of kids Josh and Sarah's age. It had been genocide, a holocaust. But *why?* There were no clues as to motive, nothing. And after a day of searching for answers, the stench and the horror overwhelmed him. So by chance he'd wandered *here* . . . to this cozy, abandoned kibbutz nestled in the hills above the Mediterranean, in the shadow of a ruined and forbidding castle built during the Crusades.

Or *was* it by chance?

The condition of the kibbutz was eerily similar to that of the barracks where he and Sarah had been separated: deserted, yet in perfect condition; stocked with food, yet stripped of weapons. The stoves and ovens worked; there was even air-conditioning. It seemed safe. He *could* have relaxed, he supposed. But he hadn't dozed longer than twenty minutes at a time since he'd arrived. He hadn't showered or changed his damp, soiled clothes. His Yankees cap was practically stuck to his head. The slightest noise, even the rustling of the wind, would set his heart racing. *This place is probably a trap,* he kept telling himself, struggling to fight the exhaustion that fogged his mind. *They probably lured me here without my knowing.*

He zipped the duffel bag shut and slung it over his shoulder, glancing out the window at the sunbaked hills and the placid blue waters of the Mediterranean. It wasn't safe here; it wasn't safe *anywhere*. But if the scene at Narahiya had accomplished one thing, it had cemented his resolve to find his sister and the scroll. He would find them or die in the act. The mysteries within mysteries, the keys to the horrors that grew every day—all lay hidden within that ancient Hebrew text. He just couldn't allow himself to think of the girls in the black robes. No, if he thought of them, he would . . . he would . . .

Did he hear something?

Josh held his breath, listening intently. Yes. *Oh, God*. He *did* hear something. Voices. His legs buckled. He had to escape. But there was only one exit—through the kitchen door and the dining area and out the front door.

He heard another sound: the creak of the front door opening.

"*Shalom,*" a voice called.

Josh gasped.

Was that *Meyer?*

"*Shalom . . .*"

His eyes widened. It *was*. "Meyer!" he shouted.

There was a pause. "Joshua?"

Baruch Hashem! The next instant Josh was slinging his duffel bag to the floor and dashing through the dining room into the front hall. He laughed. It was a miracle. Somehow Meyer and Jacob survived the ambush. A miracle! They were standing right in front of him, breathing heavily, their green uniforms stained with sweat, their machine guns drawn. Who would have thought he'd be so glad to see these two fools, his captors? He shook his head.

"You're alive," he choked. "How did you find me?"

Meyer remained stone-faced.

Jacob's fat lips curled up in a sneer. "We're soldiers,"

he snapped. *Veer soldeers.* "We're trained to track scum like you."

Josh's smile faded. "Uh . . . what?"

"You heard him," Meyer stated. He shifted the position of his machine gun so that it was pointed directly at Josh. "He said 'scum.'" The word oozed from his mouth with disgust.

"Whoa, whoa—wait a second," Josh mumbled confusedly. "Are you guys mad because I escaped—"

"Shut up!" Jacob barked.

Josh swallowed. His eyes flashed between the two of them. Their faces were cold, their jaws tight; they were *irate.* But why?

"I knew you were clever, Joshua," Meyer spat. His bald spot was red—but whether that was from the heat or from rage, Josh didn't know. "Didn't I say so? You're too smart for your age. And now I know why. You know it all."

Josh nervously licked his dry lips. "What are—"

"You tried to kill us!" Jacob shouted. He thrust the muzzle of his gun at Josh's face. "But the ambush failed. Your timing was off."

"I don't know what you're talking about," Josh breathed. "You're not making any sense. Just tell me what you think—"

"*We're* asking the questions!" Meyer interrupted. "How long have you been in league with the Black Robes?"

Josh's jaw dropped.

"Hands up!" Jacob yelled. "Above your—"

"You honestly think *I'm* with *them?*" Josh blurted, mortified. He reluctantly raised his hands. "Are you crazy? Why do you think I jumped out of the Jeep? *They're* after *me*. Why do you think I keep talking about the scroll and my sister?"

Meyer shook his head. "You jumped out of the Jeep because you knew it would explode," he murmured. "Clever, Joshua. You're a filthy, lying pig. You knew we were headed into a trap all along. And as for your sister—she's one of them, too."

"Listen, just hold on one second," Josh pleaded, struggling to remain focused. "My sister is *not* one of them. I don't even know who *they* are. Look—you left my sister to die, right? If you're so suspicious of *me*, why didn't you just leave me to die, too?"

Meyer snorted. "We *saved* you! You were smart. You took advantage of our oath to protect allies of Israel. Of course, we assumed *you* were an ally: You are an American boy. We thought the Black Robes were all girls. We thought wrong. We saved you, and you betrayed—"

"No, no, no," Josh protested. "You didn't save me. You *captured* me—"

"Silence!" Meyer commanded. "We also take an oath to eliminate enemies. Unless you want us to make good on that oath right now, you answer our questions."

Josh began to perspire feverishly. This was absurd. How could they possibly believe he was one of *them?*

"Who are the Black Robes?" Meyer growled.

"I don't *know!*" Josh cried. "All I know is that they know who *I* am, and they want my granduncle's scroll. They're trying to kill . . . Listen to me." His breathing grew strained. "They're in on this. *All* of this. I can't prove it without the scroll, but they're in on whatever killed everybody New Year's Eve. They worship somebody named Lilith, a demon or something. *Hashayd.* It's all in the scroll. That's why—"

"I've heard enough," Jacob interrupted. "I say we kill him."

Meyer nodded.

There was no time to think. Josh barreled into Jacob and shoved him off balance, then darted out the open door and into the hot sand—straight for the cliffs overlooking the ocean.

"Blee yahdieim!" Jacob yelled. "I kill you!"

Josh ducked, nearly falling flat on his face. He could hardly breathe.

Rat-tat-tat!

A quick burst of machine gun fire kicked up a cloud of dust not three feet to his left. Adrenaline shot through his body, doubling his pace. There was a huge rock ahead, right where the hill started sloping down to the cliffs. Twenty more paces, fifteen—

Rat-tat-tat!

Something sharp and hot stung Josh's arm. In a panic he glanced down and saw blood. Had he been shot? The cut wasn't deep. He had to ignore it. He sprinted behind the rock and started hastily picking his way down a steep slope.

"Stop!" Meyer's voice shouted behind him. "Joshua—stop!"

Don't listen, Josh ordered himself. *Don't look back.*

The slope gradually evened. He plowed forward. But after fifty more yards there was nowhere left to go. The earth beneath him came to a jagged end.

He skidded to a halt. He'd reached the edge of the cliff.

"Oh, God," he whispered. "Oh, God . . ."

Panting, he peered over the side. The drop must have been a hundred feet. Frothy waves gently lapped at the base of the steep wall of rock. The clear blue water didn't look that rough. But he didn't know how deep it was. At least he couldn't see the ocean floor.

"Joshua!"

That was it: all the incentive he needed.

He sucked in his breath and jumped off the cliff as far as his legs would push him.

Jackson,
Ohio
Afternoon of February 10

2/10/99

My whole life, I've always tried hard
not to hate people or things. I think
that when you hate something, you lose
some of your soul. You lose the spirit
inside that makes you special, that
makes you human. To hate is to act like
an animal.

But I finally broke down. I hate
something. I can't pretend I don't. I
hate this town and everything about it—
the booze, the airhead girls, the fact
that I know I'm never going to make it
west. And as usual, the way I feel or
what I want doesn't seem to make
one single bit of difference.

Luke is content to stay here for a long time. Maybe forever. Why not? It's perfect for him. I mean, everybody in Jackson is _so_ nice and friendly: Amanda, Laura, Rebecca, blah, blah, blah. . . . All they want to do is party. That suits Luke just fine. I'm sure he's already hooked up with one of them. I'm sure of it. At least he's forgotten about wanting to have sex with me. He's forgotten about me completely.

But I was hoping George would be different. I'm _still_ hoping.

I don't know what it is about him. Maybe it's because he saved my life. Maybe it's the way he isn't scared of Luke. Or it could be his eyes. They're so bright and green and innocent and kidlike. It's as if his eyes are trying to show people what he's really like, but he acts hard to protect himself.

And he's interested in my visions. That was obvious in the car. But why?

Does he have visions, too? Is that why he was going west?

I want to talk to him alone, but that's pretty much impossible. Those girls never leave him or Luke alone. They're always flirting, but it's more than that. It's almost like they want to keep an eye on the guys, make sure they don't do anything . . . wrong.

The girls don't pay much attention to me, though. I just sit around being bored. Last night I even got drunk for the first time in my life—I was so sick of just watching everyone else act like an idiot. I figured I might as well be an idiot, too. The girls brought us all to that huge house again. They said they were having a party to celebrate how Luke's neck is all healed. They have a party for everything. I think they want to keep the guys too drunk to notice how weird this whole place is.

I had about four glasses of wine,

and I started getting really talkative.
I wanted to know—where are all the
boys from this town? The girls said all
the boys vaporized. Whose house is
this? Rebecca's. Why do their names all
end in -a? Why do they all act like
sluts? Luke told me to shut up. The
girls just laughed it off. They told me
that my name ends in -a too. They said
I should relax—the world's gone down
the toilet, and there's nothing anybody
can do about it. We should all just get
our kicks while we can.

Sounds like a bunch of fun-loving
chicks, huh?

But I don't trust them. Sometimes
when the guys are trashed and I'm
sober, I can tell the girls aren't as
drunk as they're acting. They drink all
the time, but they're always in total
control of themselves. Like, no matter
how "drunk" they are, they always
remember to make us close our eyes

*on the way over to the house. Why?
What are they hiding? And they keep
asking George why he passed out that
day. They want to know if he " sees
things." George denies it, but I think
he's lying.*

"Julia?" a voice called.

Julia stopped writing. Somebody was upstairs. She'd nearly forgotten she was sitting right on the front steps of the mansion—right in the sun for everyone to see. That was another weird thing. Even though there was still snow on the ground and the blizzard raged whenever they went to the liquor store, it was always sunny around the mansion.

"Julia? You down there?"

Amanda. Ugh. There was no *way* Julia was going to answer her. Amanda was the worst of all: the most flirtatious, the most giggly. Julia slammed her diary shut and tucked it into her back pocket, then hopped off the front steps and tiptoed toward the woods.

"Julia?"

She heard the sound of muffled laughter drifting from a window on the second floor.

"You gotta come up here!" another voice called. "We're playing truth or dare."

Truth or dare? Julia wondered disgustedly. Why? How could they be so *happy* all the time? Didn't they care about *anything?* Didn't they care that all their parents were dead? They seemed much more interested in the fact that they now had Rebecca's house to themselves. It was sick. She picked up her pace.

"Come on, Julia!" Amanda pleaded. "Luke's here, too!"

Just leave me alone! Julia silently screamed. She broke into a jog, a run. She flew into the woods, ignoring the branches that lashed out in her path. A sudden, terrible claustrophobia consumed her. She knew that she could sprint as far as she wanted, but she'd still be trapped. She'd never escape this place. She'd never escape those girls. . . .

Finally she collapsed on her hands and knees into the wet snow in a small clearing.

What am I going to do? she wondered desperately, panting for breath. *What am I—*

Her eyes widened.

A circle of seven rough-hewn stones stood before her. Was this some kind of campground? The stones had obviously been placed there deliberately.

Very cautiously Julia pushed herself to her feet. What *was* this place?

The stones surrounded the charred, blackened remnants of what must have been a pretty huge fire. Each rock was about the size of a basketball. And each was carved with a different symbol: an owl, a snake with wings, a tree, a naked woman. . . .

The flesh on the back of her neck began to crawl.

Is this why they make us close our eyes?

She involuntarily took a step back. Something was familiar here, wasn't it? She'd seen a place like this once. But not in real life. She'd seen it in some movie . . . some movie about teenage Satanists or something.

Lord help me.

The next moment she was dashing back through the woods, slapping branches out of her way. She *knew* those girls were twisted. She *knew* it. She burst into the sunlight. . . .

Amanda stood on the porch steps, waiting for her.

Julia stopped dead in her tracks.

She knows I've seen it. She knows.

But Amanda just smiled.

"Don't you want to play truth or dare?" she asked.

**Citicorp Building,
Seattle, Washington
Night of February 14**

"So who do you think the *Chosen One* is, anyway?" Caleb asked in a spooky voice. His bloodshot blue eyes glistened in the light of the fire.

"That's not the question," Jared croaked. "The question is: Can he get us some more weed?"

Ariel giggled. She was deliciously buzzed. She felt as if she could sit here in this abandoned lobby for the rest of her life—just kicking it by the fire and picking at the dwindling mountain of soup cans . . . drinking beers, taking an occasional puff, listening to Caleb and his friends talk and joke about nothing in particular.

"Yeah, I wonder if he has a beeper number," Caleb said. "Then we wouldn't have to go to *him*—like the rest of those suckers. He could come to *us*. And he could pick up a pizza on the way. A big, greasy pepperoni pizza. With extra cheese."

"Dude, beepers don't work anymore, remember?" John piped up from behind the crackling flames. "Phones don't work, either. That's probably this guy's angle. That's why they call him the Chosen One. If you want to get stoned, you *have* to go to him."

Jared's brow grew furrowed. "What if he has Smartbeep? Wouldn't we be able to beep him if he has Smartbeep?"

"Yes," Caleb stated. He nodded sanctimoniously. "We all saw the Smartbeep commercial. They *swore* it would work, no matter what." A smile broke out on his face. "So if any of you have a defective Smartbeep beeper, now is the time to write your local distributor and demand your money-back guarantee."

Ariel grinned. The smeared, faded words *I'm a chump* still lingered on Caleb's forehead. It was adorable. He looked as if he'd used one of those temporary gag tattoos that came in Cracker Jack boxes. He'd also shaved his beard this morning, which did wonders for his appearance. He was actually a pretty decent-looking guy . . . in a goofy kind of way. He had these bushy eyebrows, a thin nose, and these really wide, thick lips—like a much younger version of the lead singer of Aerosmith.

"Whatcha thinkin', Ariel?" he asked, returning her smile. "That I have a future doing commercials for Smartbeep?"

She smirked. "No, actually I was thinking that if anybody says 'Smartbeep' again, I'm going to scream."

"Well, how about *this* for a commercial?" He suddenly leaped to his feet and threw his arms over his head. " 'It's the Men's Shirt Event you've been waiting for!' " he cried.

Ariel blinked. She struggled to maintain a straight face—but she couldn't. She started cracking up.

"Hey . . . um, Caleb?" Jared mumbled sarcastically. "Didn't I tell you not to put PCP in your Chunky beef stew?"

"What the hell is a 'Men's Shirt Event'?" John demanded.

Caleb flopped back down on the floor like a marionette whose strings had just been cut. "Come on, you guys," he groaned. "Don't you remember? That was the last thing we saw on TV before the blackout."

John and Jared exchanged a quick glance. A flash of recognition appeared on their haggard faces.

"Oh, my God—that's right," Jared moaned. "I can't believe you *remember* that."

"How could I forget?" Caleb muttered—and for the first time all night his tone was serious. He hugged his knees to his chest and turned to the fire. "It was a pretty major event in our lives."

Ariel stared at him. *Poor Caleb,* she found herself thinking. His eyes were so red and puffy. Maybe all the alcohol had altered her perceptions slightly—but he seemed so *sad* all of a sudden, like a lonely little puppy.

"What were you guys doing when it happened?" she asked.

Caleb lifted his shoulders. "We were at a party at Cynthia's house. Her brother was . . . he was sitting right next to me." He clucked his tongue. "One second he was there, and the next second he was gone." He shifted his gaze to Ariel. "How about you? What were you doing?"

"I was having a party," she mumbled. "It was me, Brian, and some other people." She swallowed. "The first person I saw melt was my dad."

Nobody said anything for a moment.

Whoops, Ariel thought. Maybe she should have kept that last part to herself. Now the vibe in here was really gloomy. The silence stretched on. The sound of the crackling flames filled the vast, empty room. All at once she found that *she* was just as bummed out as these guys. This was no good. Everybody needed some cheering up, pronto. *No more negativity,* she reminded herself. There had to be something positive about what happened on New Year's Eve. There *had* to be.

"Just look at it this way, Caleb," Ariel finally said, in total earnestness. "At least there won't ever be another such thing as a 'Men's Shirt Event,' right?"

Caleb grinned.

"What?" Ariel asked. She glanced around the room.

Jared started to chuckle . . . and then he shook his head. Caleb was laughing, too. So was John.

Before Ariel knew it, the four of them were rolling around on the rug in hysterics.

"Men's Shirt Event!" Caleb hooted wildly. "Men's—"

"Hey," a quiet voice interrupted. "What's going on?"

Uh-oh. Ariel bolted upright. Brian stood staring at them. He must have just walked in. And he was holding something in his hands, something cone shaped . . . *flowers?*

"Hey!" Caleb cried, struggling to get a grip on himself. A few last giggles managed to escape his lips. "Where have you been, bro?"

"I've been out," Brian answered hesitantly. "Just wandering around." He surveyed the four of them, his face wrinkled in confusion. Finally his eyes came to rest on Ariel. "Ariel, can I talk to you for a second?" he murmured.

Ariel shrugged. "I'm all ears, baby."

For some reason that sent Caleb, Jared, and John right into another fit of crazed laughter. Ariel bit her lip in an effort to keep control of herself.

"Alone?" Brian asked, staring at her. His jaw was tight.

She frowned. "What's the problem?"

"It's just . . ." He shifted on his feet, glaring at the three other boys. "Can you just come with me for a second?"

The laughter stopped.

Ariel sighed. Perfect. Now Brian was embarrassing himself–*and* her. "I don't think I should stand, Bri," she stated flatly. "I'm pretty wasted. I was actually thinking about having a smoke." She glanced at Caleb. "Think I can bum a cigarette?"

Caleb patted his jeans pockets. "I'm pretty sure I'm out. . . ."

"You don't *smoke,*" Brian told her.

"Who says?" she grumbled. She turned back to him, growing more irritable by the second. "So what do you want, anyway?"

Brian grimaced, then thrust the flowers at her. "I got you these."

For a few seconds Ariel simply gaped at the wilted gaggle of roses clenched in his fist. "Why?" she finally asked.

"Why?" he snapped. "Why? Because you've been blowing me off for weeks–ever since you lost your

stupid porno book and your underwear. But we're supposed to be in this together, remember? We love each other. And that *matters*, Ariel."

Ariel's face turned bright red. *Oh, Jesus.* He sounded like a Hallmark card written by Charles Manson. Couldn't he see that he was making a total fool out of himself? Caleb and the others must think she was the biggest loser on the planet.

"Love matters," Caleb mused in the awkward silence. "Cute."

But Ariel was seething. It wasn't cute at all. It was incredibly lame. *Love matters?* Did Brian really think that a bunch of dead *flowers* was going to make up for the fact that she'd lost the only tangible reminders she had of her former life? Of her father? Didn't he understand that losing that stuff was his fault? *That* was what mattered.

"And in case you forgot, it's Valentine's Day," Brian added. "Happy Valentine's Day."

He paused—clearly waiting for her to say something.

Ariel snatched the flowers out of his hand.

She tossed them into the fire.

Brian gasped.

"Happy Valentine's Day to you, too, Bri," she growled. "Sorry to harsh your mellow, but in the future, try to keep in mind that what I *really* want on this lovely corporate holiday is a pack of cigarettes and an illustrated history of erotic film. Got it?"

ELEVEN

**Jackson,
Ohio
Night of February 19**

One night—George wasn't even sure *which* night—he sat slumped on the soft leather couch in the living room of Rebecca's mansion, staring at a few crackling logs in the marble fireplace. His gut felt as if it were rotting from the inside out. His head didn't feel much better, either. Luckily he was alone. Amanda and a few other girls were upstairs. The rest were at the liquor store with Luke. George needed some time to himself. He needed a break—from drinking, from partying, from *everything.*

How long had he even *been* in this town? A week? Two weeks? He couldn't tell anymore. One day tumbled into the next in a drunken blur. He didn't understand how those girls could do it, night after night. Their stomachs must be made of iron or something.

Tonight I'm not gonna drink, he promised himself. *Tonight I'm just gonna go to sleep.*

At least he hadn't had any more flashes since that one time. Maybe they were going away. It was possible, wasn't it?

No. If the visions were going away, then he wouldn't still need to go west. He wouldn't wake up every morning feeling as if he were trapped in quick-sand, as if every minute that he stayed in one place were a mistake. He *had* to go west. He tried to fight it, but no matter how drunk he got, he still felt the need to travel.

Amanda kept asking him if he had visions. She must have known he was lying. But he had to make her believe him—otherwise he had no hope of scamming on her. Anyway, it felt good to deny the truth. He didn't want to admit it to *himself* anymore. More than anything he wanted to forget about the Demon, and the Chosen One, and his baby with the beautiful eyes. Life could be so sweet here in Jackson if he forgot. So sweet.

Still, this very evening he'd taken the car for a spin and stared into the western sky. It had taken all his concentration just to turn the car around the other way. The setting sun burned the back of his neck like an accusation.

"George?" a voice whispered.

He sat up with a start. Julia was standing in the hall. He hadn't even heard her come in. Before he could say a word, she put a finger over her lips to indicate silence.

"What?" he mouthed, wrinkling his brow.

She waved for him to follow her. He chewed his lip, then stood. What did she want? She'd barely said two words to him since they'd met.

Oh, well. He limped after her. On his way out the door he caught a glimpse of himself in the hallway mirror. Brother, did he look like crap. Huge purple sacks hung under his eyes. The platinum dye had nearly washed out of his hair, leaving it a dull blond—his natural color. His face seemed bloated. He *had* to quit drinking so much.

"Follow me," Julia whispered.

They tiptoed down the steps and into the frigid night air. It wasn't snowing, but the temperature had dropped sharply since the sun went down. George angrily flipped the collar of his black leather jacket up around his neck. It was too cold to be messing around outside in the dark.

"Where are we going?" he demanded. He could see his breath.

"Somewhere we can talk. Alone."

A nervous twitter passed through his stomach. *I bet she wants to talk about the voices she hears.*

He swallowed. He didn't want to get into this. Not now. He wanted to forget.

"This way," she murmured. She tugged gently at his jacket and led him into a narrow, snowy path through the woods. Waterlogged branches swatted his body and scratched his face, but she kept going. He glanced over his shoulder. The trees were so thick that he could hardly see the house anymore.

"I don't think anybody can hear us," he mumbled.

After a few more steps she stopped and turned around.

"George, this is important," she said quietly.

He shrugged. "Um, okay." They stood face-to-face, only about a foot apart. They were too close; it made him bothered, anxious. He squinted at her soft features. Gradually his vision adjusted to the dim light.

She took a deep breath. "Okay, this is gonna sound weird." She looked down at her feet and kicked at the snow.

"You want to know if I see things, right?" he asked reluctantly.

Her head shot up. "Do you?"

"Yeah." He sighed. In a weird way, he felt relieved. It wasn't *so* bad. He supposed he had to talk to *somebody* about this stuff—or else he'd go crazy.

"I *knew* it," she breathed. "What do you see?"

"I, uh . . ." He gave one short laugh, then lowered his gaze. His face grew flushed. A big part of the reason he wanted to forget about the visions was because they were so damn embarrassing. He saw a baby—*his* baby—but he'd barely ever gotten to second base with a girl. Not that he would admit that to *her*, of course.

"You first," he mumbled. "You hear voices, right?"

"No, I see myself in a desert," she said breathlessly. "And I see myself stabbing a demon."

George glanced up. "I see the Demon, too, sometimes," he said quietly.

Her face brightened. She looked so *happy*. And he knew exactly how she felt. It was like finding a soul mate. He'd felt the same way when he'd talked to that guy Doug, the guy who'd rescued him from jail. It was pretty nice to learn that you weren't the only person in the world who was losing your mind.

Of course, Doug melted after he told George about the visions. Just the way Amanda described what happened to that guy she knew.

"Do you see the Chosen One?" Julia pressed.

100

He shook his head. "Uh-uh. No."

"Me neither. But I know that the Chosen One is out west somewhere. I don't *see* it, but somehow I just know. It's like there's some huge magnet pulling me out there, pulling me toward the Chosen One."

"Yeah, me too," he said. "That's why—"

"You were going west," she finished. She stepped closer. "But you got sidetracked."

He shrugged. "I guess. But—"

"George, listen to me," she interrupted. Her voice grew forceful, urgent. "We gotta get out of this place. I mean, I know life is cushy here, with the house and the booze and the girls and all, but, but . . ." She shook her head. "Look, forget it. There's just some weird stuff going on around here, okay?"

He frowned. "What kind of stuff?"

"I don't even know. All I know is that we have to keep going. *You* know it. *I* know it. We're wasting time. We should leave. The two of us. Tonight."

He cocked an eyebrow. "You wanna just split?"

"Why not?"

"But . . . uh, what about Luke?"

She laughed bitterly. "What about him?"

"Well, I don't know him too well, but I got a feeling he isn't gonna like being ditched." He smirked. "Aren't you two, like, you know . . . a couple or something?"

"We *were,*" she muttered. "Anyway, it's not like he can follow us. You've got the car. He's passed out at the store right now. We can just get in and go."

George hesitated. He couldn't believe this. A gorgeous girl—an older girl, no less—was trying to ditch her boyfriend for *him*. Okay, she didn't want to fool around with him or anything . . . but still, she wanted to travel alone. That was *something*. On the other hand, he was ill and exhausted. Driving was the last thing he wanted to do, especially in the snow. Plus he'd be leaving behind food and shelter and a boat-load of fun-loving females. He stared at Julia. He could feel the seconds silently ticking by.

The visions would never go away; he *knew* that.

And as long as there were visions, there was no chance he'd ever hook up with Amanda.

His heart seemed to flutter. He reached into his pocket for his car keys. "Okay . . ."

"Wait!" Julia whispered. Her face suddenly went blank. She was looking at something over George's shoulder.

Wet leaves rustled behind them.

Uh-oh. George spun around, half expecting to see Luke.

"Hey, guys!"

Amanda. He breathed a quick sigh of relief.

Amanda's eyes glittered in the moonlight. She was wearing a sexy black spaghetti-strap dress. He tried not to stare at her.

"What are you doing out here?" she asked with a smile. But there was something different about her smile, something that made George feel even colder than he already was.

He turned to Julia, hoping she would come up with a quick excuse. She didn't.

"You know that this is where we make you close your eyes, right?" Amanda asked.

Make us close our eyes? George's breath caught in his throat. *That* was a weird thing to say. Closing his eyes was just a little game Amanda played . . . wasn't it?

"It's freezing. Don't you guys think you better come in?"

Julia stepped forward. "Actually, we—"

"Oh, you know what, George?" Amanda cut in. "I meant to tell you. Two of your tires are flat." She laughed. "You must have run over some bottles."

George stared at her in confusion. He hadn't run over any bottles. He hadn't run over *anything.*

"It's a drag, I know," Amanda said in that same easygoing tone, as if answering an unspoken question. "None of us have cars, and there aren't any gas stations for miles."

He studied her uneasily. "So what are you saying?"

She shrugged. Her chilly smile widened. "Nothing. You're just stuck with us for a while, that's all. Maybe a *long* while."

"But—"

"But what?" she interrupted. "You do like it here, George. Don't you?"

PART III

February 20

TWELVE

Citicorp Building,
Seattle, Washington
Morning of February 20

Ariel stood by one of the floor-to-ceiling windows of the lobby, staring blankly at the sky. After weeks of snow, this morning it had suddenly stopped. The temperature had risen at least fifty degrees—everywhere she looked, all she saw was runny gray slush. She'd never seen snow melt so fast. And now there were the clouds—thick greenish storm clouds slowly covering the city. If it weren't February, Ariel would say they were in for the mother of all summer thunderstorms. *Man.* This weather was getting freaky.

Ariel shook her head and turned away from the window. She had to get out of here for a while—at least to look for Brian. He'd left yesterday morning and still hadn't returned.

A fleeting pang of guilt flashed through her.

Am I a total bitch?

Yeah. Sure she was. But Brian knew that. So why was he still giving her the silent treatment? He'd been giving her the silent treatment ever since Valentine's Day. Okay, maybe she *had* been a little harsh. But she deserved to be a bitch every once in a while, didn't she? *Everybody* did. It wasn't as if she could talk to a shrink or take some Prozac or anything. For Christ's sake, she was squatting in an office building for a home. Her father was dead, and her best friend was shacked up with Ariel's psychotic brother. The brother who'd threatened to kill Ariel if she ever came near him again. She'd been living on nothing but beer and soup for practically three weeks. Three weeks! She was *bound* to go a little nuts.

"Hey, Ariel?" Caleb called. "You wanna play a game with us?"

Ariel glanced over her shoulder at the fire. *Jeez.* It was starting to get kind of crowded in here. She shook her head—then found herself laughing. The scene in this lobby was getting to be a lot like the scene she'd left behind in Babylon: Namely, there was a drunken posse growing bigger by the day. About ten kids had wandered into the building since Valentine's Day, and none of them had left.

Some of them were Caleb's friends. Some weren't.

She sighed. At least none of them were looking for the "Chosen One." Or if they were, they were keeping it to themselves.

"Come on, Ariel," Caleb prodded. His smiling face glowed orange in the flickering light. He raised his thick eyebrows suggestively. "It's gonna be fun. . . ."

A tired grin curled her lips. "Oh, yeah?" she called. "What is it?"

"It's called end of the world," somebody replied.

Caleb nodded. He beckoned to her with a beer bottle.

"End of the world, huh?" she muttered. Rolling her eyes, she trudged across the red carpet and slumped down beside Caleb. "Sounds thrilling," she said, as dully as possible. The truth, of course, was that she *was* a little intrigued. She just loved busting Caleb's chops. He always had a quick comeback. Always.

Caleb handed her a bottle of beer. "Now don't be a sourpuss," he teased.

"A *sourpuss?*" Ariel smirked at him as she twisted off the cap. "That sounds like something my grandmother would have said." She raised the bottle to her lips.

"No, wait!" Caleb cried. "This is a *drinking* game."

She shot him a withering stare. "So you won't mind if I drink."

"No. But only if you promise not to breathe until you brush your teeth," he said. "I mean, no offense, but ever since we ran out of spearmint gum . . ."

She stuck out her tongue—and the two of them started laughing.

"Okay, okay," Jared mumbled impatiently. "Listen up."

Ariel took a slug of beer. *Yuck.* She nearly spit it out. How long had this beer been sitting by the fire? It was all fizzy and hot.

"You listening, Ariel?" Jared groaned.

She nodded, placing the bottle by her side. "Yeah, yeah. End of the world. Go ahead."

"We go around the circle," he explained. "When it's your turn, you say one sentence about what you would do if it were the end of the world. Then the rest of the people vote on it to decide whether it's lame or not. If the majority says it's lame, you drink. If the majority thinks it's cool, everybody *else* drinks."

Ariel blinked. Was it just her—or did that make

absolutely no sense? She glanced at Caleb, then at the rest of the kids huddled around the fire. They looked totally baffled.

"Um, Jared?" she asked. "What's to prevent everybody from voting 'lame' every time?"

"Nothing," he said matter-of-factly. "Either way, everybody gets drunk. Besides, since it actually *is* the end of the world, it's in our best interest to come up with something cool."

"Touché," Ariel said with a smile. She shrugged. "Well. Sounds good to me." She took another swig of hot beer. This time it didn't taste so bad.

Jared leaned back and pointed a finger at Caleb. "You first, dude."

"Me first." Caleb stared into the fire and stroked his chin, pretending to be thoughtful. "Well, if it were the end of the world . . . I think I would do what I've always dreamed of doing. I would watch every single episode of *The World's Deadliest Car Chases* back to back, in order, while eating a six-foot meatball sub. Then my heart would explode."

Ariel paused. *"Boooo!"* she chanted. *"Booo!"*

The rest of the circle immediately joined in: *"Booo!"*

She giggled and thrust her bottle at Caleb. "Drink up, champ." She winked at Jared. "I kind of like this game."

Caleb guzzled half the beer in one gulp.

"What about you, Ariel?" Jared asked. "Now it's your turn. What would you do?"

"Me?" She shook her head. "I gotta think—"

"Ariel?" a harsh, gravelly voice interrupted from behind her.

She swiveled around. Her jaw dropped.

110

"Brian?" she cried. She stumbled off the floor and ran over to him. God. He looked *awful*. He'd lost his jacket, and his clothes were torn—clear through to the skin. He was as pale as a sheet and breathing heavily. His face seemed drawn, as if he hadn't slept.

"What happened to you?" she whispered. "Where have you *been?*"

"I don't have time to explain," he panted. "Look. There's a bus waiting for us a couple of blocks away. I told the—"

"Whoa, whoa, slow down," she murmured. "A bus?"

"There's no time to slow down, all right?" He jerked his head toward the door. "They're *waiting* for us. I barely convinced the guy who's driving. A bunch of kids are going to California. They said they could give us a lift. But we have to leave *now.*"

She managed a wry smile. Obviously he was in a state of shock. He just needed to mellow out for a second, to get himself together.

"Come on!" he barked.

"So I guess you're talking to me now, huh?" she asked quietly. "The silent treatment's over?"

Brian gripped her shoulders. "Ariel, I don't have time for this. We can work out our problems later. But right now you're getting on that bus."

Ariel returned his stare. Her smile vanished, and with it, her concern. Brian had never ordered her around before. Ever. *Nobody* ordered her around. But now Brian was telling her to get on some strange bus with some strange kids—a bunch of kids he didn't even know—just because they *said* they were going to California. Right.

111

"Brian, I'm not gonna go without *thinking* about it," she stated.

"Jesus!" Brian jerked his hands away from her and threw them over his head. "They're *leaving,* Ariel! Right this second! Don't you get it?"

She frowned. "Yeah, I get it. Loud and clear."

Brian turned and began pacing in tight circles. "What's it gonna be?" he asked, avoiding her eyes. "I have to know. Now."

Ariel hesitated. She glanced back at the fire. Everybody was gawking at her.

"Come on, Ariel," Caleb called, wearing that same goofy grin. "It's your turn."

"Ariel!" Brian snapped.

She turned back to him. Her mind started racing. Well. This was quite a predicament. If he wanted her to make such a drastic decision with no time, she'd just have to make a game out of it. Better yet—a *drinking* game.

"Lemme ask you something, Bri," she said calmly. "If it were the end of the world, what would you do?"

"What?" he cried. His face darkened—then he rubbed his eyes and took a deep breath, as if trying to calm himself. "It *is* the end of the world, Ariel," he said in a shaky voice. "And I'm telling you what I'm doing. I'm going to someplace better. That bus is our ticket to a new life, okay? We're going to go south until it gets warm up here again. And then we're gonna deal with Trevor. Remember? It's our plan. We're gonna make the world a better place."

Ariel shook her head. *Wrong answer,* she thought. At *least* he could have said that he'd try to get his hands on another copy of *Skin Tight.* Going south

112

was never *her* plan, anyway. Besides, compared to what Caleb had said, Brian's response was downright pathetic. She'd much rather eat a six-foot hero than help Brian save the world.

"I think you better go without me," she proclaimed.

He studied her for a second, his face void of expression.

Then he bolted outside. The glass door slammed behind him.

Ariel blinked. *Wow.*

That had been quite a little freak-out, hadn't it? How long had that whole scene even lasted? Things were happening *way* too fast around here.

But Brian would be back any second. There was no way he could have just run out that door and out of her life forever.

No way.

A flash of brilliant blue-white light forked through the sky, followed by the loudest peal of thunder Ariel had ever heard. The storm clouds burst open, rain falling in sheets so thick, she couldn't even see across the street. Within seconds Brian's form disappeared into the pouring water.

"Ariel?" Caleb came up beside her and stared out at the rain. "It's your turn."

She glanced up into his bloodshot eyes. Another flash of lightning illuminated the lobby.

"If it were the end of the world, what would you do?" he asked softly.

Ariel swallowed down the lump in her throat. "I'd get so drunk that I couldn't remember what my father looked like."

THIRTEEN

Jackson,
Ohio
February 20

The desert sun is right above me. It's wearing me down, but I have to stay strong. The Demon is circling me in the sand. It laughs at me and bellows with flame, its terrible red eyes fixed upon my sword. I have to plan my attack carefully. I have to stab it when the moment is—

"Julia!"

Her eyes popped open. She took a deep breath. She was drenched in sweat, lying in the dark. For some reason George was standing above her. He bent down and grasped her shoulders. His fingers dug into her flesh so hard that it hurt.

Uh-oh. Even with the merest bit of light, she could tell that something was wrong. George was chewing his lips; his eyes were unsteady. He looked scared. George *never* looked scared. This was bad. Had he found that place in the woods? Had he seen something awful? He must have. . . .

"Come on," he whispered. He pulled her roughly to her feet. It took a groggy moment for her to realize that she'd fallen asleep in one of the liquor store aisles.

"We're outta here," he stated.

Before she could utter a word of protest, he pushed her toward the front door. She stumbled once, trying to get her bearings. The place was absolutely deserted. Had it been deserted when she'd fallen asleep? No, it hadn't. The girls hadn't left her alone for one single second since the day she'd seen the stone circle.

"Where is everyone?" she managed to ask.

"No idea," he muttered. "And I'm not gonna wait around to find out."

He shoved her through the door and out into the night. The sky was pitch-black, thick clouds covering the stars. Julia wrapped her arms around herself. Her ratty wool coat seemed to provide less and less protection every time she went outside. She shivered—partly from the sudden breeze and partly from growing fear.

"What's up?" she murmured. "Why are we leaving?"

George limped hurriedly beside her, steering her into the woods. He glanced over his shoulder before he spoke. "You were right," he finally said. "There's something bad going on here. Those girls lied to me."

Julia's heart skipped a beat. "Wh-what did they do?" she stammered, batting aside some branches as she followed him into the thick tangle of trees.

"First of all, somebody slashed the tires on my car," he breathed in a tremulous voice. "I didn't run over any bottles."

"I figured," Julia whispered. She fought to remain calm—crouching as she walked, clumsily trying to avoid the brush that George absently allowed to swing back in her face. "I bet it was Luke. I bet he did it so we wouldn't be able to leave."

"Maybe," George muttered. "Would he steal my gun, too?"

Julia cringed. "Somebody stole your gun?"

"I noticed it was missing when I woke up yesterday," he went on. "It totally freaked me out. Then I decided to check out that place where Amanda told us to close our eyes." The words poured from his mouth in a rapid monotone. "There was this fire pit there and a circle of stones carved with all kinds of weird symbols. I think those girls are into devil worship or something."

"I know," she muttered.

He stopped for a second, spinning to face her. "You *know?* Why didn't you tell me?"

"I wanted to," she whispered. "I was going to tell you the other night—but then Amanda snuck up on us."

"So what do you think it means?" he asked, wiping the sweat off his face with his sleeve.

She shrugged. "I don't know. What do *you* think? What else did you see?"

He shook his head. "Nothing," he mumbled. He plowed through the brush again.

Julia sighed, following right behind him. Oddly enough, she felt a peculiar kind of relief. So he'd seen the same thing—and nothing more. She'd been expecting him to say that he'd found a bunch of dead bodies, or instruments of torture, or *something* more dangerous and threatening than the fire pit. She could handle the fire pit. *Barely,* but she could handle it. At least neither of them had seen any evidence that the girls were violent.

"So where are we going?" she whispered after him.

He snickered. "See, that's another thing they lied about. They said there wasn't another car for miles. But tonight I found a pickup truck right up here on a dirt road. We're taking it and getting the hell out of here."

Julia nodded. They were leaving. That was all that mattered.

"There it is!" George pointed.

He scampered forward and vanished behind a tree trunk. Julia staggered after him. A moment later she found herself on a rough path that cut the woods in half. And sure enough, the shadowy hulk of an old pickup truck was waiting there in the night, as if it had been placed there just for them. Its wheels were embedded deep in the slush of melting snow.

"The keys oughta be right inside," he mumbled, pressing his face against the window. He jiggled the door handle—but the door seemed stuck.

Julia swallowed.

A gust of wind blew, sweeping strands of tangled hair across her face. Suspicion began to creep into her mind. What if the truck *had* been placed there just for them? Their escape was working out a little *too* well. Wouldn't it have been very, very careless for the girls to leave this truck so close to the liquor store, with the keys in the ignition?

"George," she whispered. "George, maybe—"

"Going somewhere, Jules?"

Luke!

Julia stiffened. Her legs seemed to give out from under her, and she collapsed against George.

Luke stepped out of the shadows and stood before them, with Amanda at his side.

"You wouldn't be trying to steal my truck, would you?" Amanda asked.

Julia's eyes flashed to Amanda's right hand. She was holding something, a stick. For a horrible moment Julia was certain that the girl was going to clobber her over the head with it. But Amanda just smiled, then reached into her pocket and pulled out a lighter. She clicked on a flame. It seemed to struggle in the wind until she waved it over the tip of her stick—and the tip leaped alive with a *whoosh* of fire.

Julia squinted into the night.

All the girls are here!

Her blood ran cold. In the dim light she could see a line of silhouettes stretching back into the woods behind Luke. Amanda turned and lit another torch. The girl behind her did the same, as did the next, and so on . . . down the row the flame went—one torch after another like tumbling dominoes: *whoosh, whoosh, whoosh* . . . until thirty flames illuminated the truck, the woods, and the road in a hellish red glow.

"By the way, the keys aren't in the truck," Amanda said.

"Wha-what?" Julia stuttered.

"Why not?" George asked.

A wicked smile crossed Amanda's lips. "I took them out. I knew you'd come looking for them. But I wouldn't lie to you, George."

She took a step forward, holding the torch like a weapon. "Like I told you before, you're stuck with us. No one leaves here."

FOURTEEN

Desert of Northeast Egypt,
Near the Israeli Border
Evening of February 20

Sarah Levy stumbled over the crest of the sand dune and breathed a hoarse sigh of dreamy relief. The sun had finally fallen below the horizon. *Finally.* A brilliant swath of fiery orange light now divided the endless blue above her from the endless white of the desert.

No more daylight. No more sun to bake every last drop of moisture from her body. No more rays to burn her flesh.

She ran a dry tongue over cracked and swollen lips. She couldn't stop staring up at the sky. When had it gotten so terribly hot? And *why?* Even in the desert it was supposed to get cold at night, wasn't it? But the unbearable heat had lasted all through the nights. How long could it stay this way? Would it be this hot forever?

The heavy knapsack on her back pulled at her, and she swayed once—but she didn't look down. A few wisps of greasy brown hair fell in her face. The sunset out here was so dazzling, even through the blurred and soiled lenses of her glasses. So impossibly beautiful . . .

"Whoa!" she croaked.

The ground seemed to drop away from her. She lost her footing and tumbled forward, scraping her raw, scorched knees in the sand. The knapsack fell off her back with a thud. There was some pain—but the pain was far away, remote. No, actually . . . the sand felt *good* against her warm skin. Nice and cool. She dug her hands deep beneath the surface and allowed the little granules to flow through her fingers.

Ahhh.

The sensation was amazing. Like dipping her hands in water. She closed her eyes for a moment, envisioning herself in a swimming pool, sipping a tall glass of—

"Stop it!" she hissed out loud.

Her sticky eyelids popped open. *Stupid,* she scolded herself. She couldn't allow herself to day-dream about water. It would drive her insane. But her parched throat involuntarily struggled to swallow. She suddenly realized that she'd had her last drop of liquid—a warm gulp of sour orange juice—yesterday morning. Thirty-six hours ago. Two full days of being in the raw heat of the deep desert with nothing to drink.

"My journal," she whispered. "Gotta write in my journal."

She'd almost forgotten about it. She had to write. Writing was key. Writing would take her mind off the temperature and the thirst. She clumsily shifted her position so she was sitting cross-legged in the sand, then snatched the heavy black knapsack into her lap. Her hands shook as she fumbled with the zipper. Why hadn't she written? She hadn't opened her journal since she'd fled Jerusalem over three weeks ago. She'd hardly even opened her knapsack.

But there was a reason, of course. A secret reason.

She didn't want to have to lay her eyes on what else was in there.

"Gotta write in my journal," she repeated, a little more desperately. Her whispery voice floated on the hot desert wind.

Averting her gaze, she shoved her hand inside the bag and felt for her spiral notebook. Her fingers brushed against leathery parchment. *No!* She jerked her hand away and frowned. Where was her notebook, anyway? *There*—buried at the bottom of the bag. With a small grunt she wrenched it free and yanked out the pen stuck in the binding.

Been in the desert for days now. Heading west. Hoping to come to the coast but must have accidentally turned south. I think I'm in Egypt. Still no closer to figuring out why those girls in black robes blew up Elijah's house. Still have no idea who they are, how they know so much about our family, or why they wanted

the scroll. Wondering if the
boys who took Josh are
connected to them. The barracks
where we stayed must have
been a trap. Wondering if
Josh is still

Sarah drew in a sharp breath. She squeezed her
eyes shut. A tight, hot sensation gripped her chest.
She fought to ignore it. She couldn't allow herself to
think about her brother for too long.

Wondering if Josh is still
alive. Where is he? Is he
thinking about the scroll? He
says it has some kind of
power. Maybe it does. After
the solar flare and the
melting people and those evil
girls who know about our
family, I'm prepared to believe
almost anything. But I'm too
frightened to read the scroll.
It scares me. Josh said there
are prophecies, something
about the weather and the

earth suffering with a Chosen One. That's the kind of garbage I never believed in before. But what if it's true? I keep thinking of what Josh said about the scroll: "It's not going to kill you." But those girls, those guys with guns —they might have killed Josh for the scroll. What is the code that Josh and Elijah talked about? Maybe if I decipher the code, the scroll can help me. Please, God.

A teardrop fell from Sarah's cheek. Her body quivered. She shook her head, angry for wasting her own precious moisture on *crying*, angry for speculating about things she didn't understand, angry for praying. Prayer had never done anybody a bit of good. She *knew* that. Deeds were what counted, not the words of a useless religion.

Maybe that was why she was so mad. Her deeds had gotten her nowhere. She'd lost her own flesh and blood. She'd lost her little brother—maybe the only other Levy left alive on this earth. And if he were dead, she had nobody to blame but herself. She hadn't allowed herself to face that horrible truth until now, but there it was. It was indisputable. He'd never survive alone. He was smart—*brilliant*, in fact—but too frail. He wouldn't last.

Why had she run when those soldiers took him? Well, that was easy: She was a coward. Not only that, she was a *stupid* coward. She'd scrambled into the desert with just a bottle of juice and a scroll that weighed about a million tons. *Stupid, stupid, stupid!* She should have tried to follow the guys who took her brother. That would have been the *responsible* thing to do. Maybe Josh was still in Jerusalem. It was a possibility, right?

Yes. She blinked a few times. She *was* going to go back to Jerusalem. Right this second. The western sky was starting to turn a pinkish red, but there would be plenty of light for a little while longer. Her eyes wandered back in the direction of Israel. . . .

What on earth is that?

There was something wrong with the sky in the east. It looked blotchy, as if it were covered with clouds. Clouds in the desert? She used her sandy T-shirt to wipe her glasses clean. *Good God!*

There *were* clouds. A dark, gray, billowy mass was sweeping westward toward the sunset, spreading across the blue expanse like a massive puddle of spilled paint.

I must be delirious, she said to herself. *Those look like storm clouds.*

Yes. She was obviously hallucinating. Dehydration was driving her mad. There were no storm clouds in the desert.

Thunder rumbled somewhere in the distance. She shook her head. All right. In reality, she was probably dying. It wasn't a big surprise. She wasn't even all that afraid. She was too tired to feel much of anything. If she regained consciousness, she would most likely find herself lying facedown in the desert, surrounded by vultures.

Wouldn't she?

Wind rustled her hair—a powerful wind that grew and grew and grew until her clothes were flapping. Specks of sand stung her skin and her eyes. Once more, Sarah squinted up at the sky. It was almost completely concealed by a thick layer of storm clouds now. The air was rapidly darkening, thickening. . . . It felt like soup. She couldn't believe it. Did *everyone* experience this sort of craziness when they were dying of thirst?

She shoved her notebook back into her knapsack, then slung the bag over her shoulder and forced herself to her feet. In the eerie gray twilight a few drops of rain began to splatter the earth around her. They fell in a jerky rhythm, dotting the white sand with scattered splotches.

Incredible. She felt the droplets on her skin. There were worse ways to go, she supposed. She just never imagined that the delirium before death would be so *vivid.*

The rain grew more intense. She lifted her arms and looked at herself, laughing. She was getting drenched! Soaked! It felt so real! Summoning what was left of her strength, she cupped her hands. They rapidly filled with water. She brought them to her lips and slurped. Wondrous coolness flowed through her body. It was paradise.

Maybe Elijah was right, she thought with a wistful grin. *Maybe there* is *an afterlife.*

Her knees buckled.

Uh-oh.

The water slipped through her fingers. Her head was swimming. Something was wrong with her. In addition to the pattering roar of the rain she could hear this strange noise, a weird kind of rhythmic thumping. . . .

It was right behind her, as a matter of fact. And it was getting louder. *Fast.*

Sarah whirled around—just in time to see several huge shadows sweep over the crest of the sand dune.

Jesus!

The soaked earth trembled. She wanted to scream, but her throat wouldn't work. Voices shouted in the downpour. A few bewildered moments passed before Sarah realized that she was being surrounded by horses . . . so many . . . horses mounted by figures in flowing cloaks and turbans. Dark eyes stared out from faces wrapped in plaid scarves.

Arabs. Arab nomads.

She wasn't dying, was she? No. She was very much alive. This was *real*—the storm, the horsemen, all of it. . . .

The Arabs slowed to a stop, forming a perfect circle around her, blocking any escape. There must have been a dozen of them at least. Their horses wheezed and snorted, shifting on their hooves in the wet sand. A cold dread settled over Sarah's body. She'd just come from Jerusalem—where teenage Arabs were slaughtering teenage Jews in the streets and vice versa. Did they know she was Jewish? She certainly couldn't pass for an Arab, not with her blue jeans and T-shirt and American hairstyle—

"Mahrhaba," one of the horsemen called.

Sarah stood perfectly still. Her heart was pounding. She thought it might burst. Why hadn't she bothered to learn Arabic? All she knew how to do was order a falafel sandwich. Big help. She gazed at the horseman who had spoken. He was shaking his head at her, squinting at her through the rain, *studying* her. What was he thinking? That he wanted to kill her? Torture her? Make her his slave?

"Al-hamdu Lillah!" he shouted, his voice booming. He laughed once. *"Al-hamdu Lillah!"*

A gasp rose from the rest of the crowd.

The horseman tightened his reins. Sarah took a step back in the wet sand. Her legs weakened under the strain of the knapsack. *Please don't hurt me.*

"Hai!" he yelled, kicking with his ankles.

Sarah flinched.

In a blur the horse bolted straight at her, nostrils flaring.

The pounding of hooves filled her ears.

"Help me!" she cried.

But before the words had fully passed her lips, her head started spinning, and the wet earth opened and swallowed her into a black abyss.

FIFTEEN

Jackson,
Ohio
February 20

Julia couldn't move. She stared into the sea of flickering torches, too frightened to even breathe. George wrapped his arms around her, as if trying to shield her from the terror of those smiling female faces.

"What the hell do you want, anyway?" he snapped at Amanda. "Who are you people?"

Amanda just shook her head. "No, George. The question is: Who are *you?*"

"I told you who I am," he snapped. "I have nothing to hide. *You're* the liars, not me."

"Bull," Luke spat.

George jumped forward—but Julia tugged on his leather jacket to stop him. Even in her petrified state, there was no way she would allow George to get himself hurt. No way.

Amanda chuckled softly. "You're a brave boy, George. But you *are* a liar. You keep claiming that you don't see things. But your friend Luke told us otherwise. See, when we were playing truth or dare, he told us something interesting. He told us that you *do* have visions." She tilted her head. "Doesn't 'the Demon' ring any bells?"

131

Julia gasped. The Demon! Luke told them about . . . they knew *everything!*

"You *bastard!*" she shrieked.

"Julia, please," Amanda murmured. She sounded amused. "Why the fuss? We asked you to play, but you didn't want to." She paused, then nodded. "Oh . . . I get it. You have something to hide. You see things, too."

"I told you she doesn't see things," Luke growled. "Only *he* does."

"But you're *also* a liar, Luke," Amanda replied. She kept her gaze fixed on Julia.

Julia's throat tightened. In a flash the whole scenario became perfectly clear: Luke wanted to get rid of George. *Only* George. So he'd betrayed him to these psychopaths—and lied about Julia. It was beyond sick; it was beyond depraved; it was beyond anything he'd ever done.

Luke lowered his eyes, sheepishly fingering the scar on his neck.

Rat! Julia thought disgustedly. Her body trembled. Fury burned inside her. *You rat!*

"You *are* a Visionary, Julia," Amanda announced, raising her voice. "And all Visionaries must die."

"*What?*" Luke shook his head. "I thought . . ."

"Shut up!" Julia screamed. She couldn't bear to hear him talk. She wrenched herself free from George. Her legs seemed to leap forward of their own free will. She found herself tackling Luke, hurtling him into a snowbank, savagely scratching at his face. His shocked blue eyes filled her entire field of vision, and the fear she saw there intoxicated her, delighted her, fed the energy of attack. She was no longer aware of any danger—only a desire to hurt, to maim, to *kill.*

"Stop it!" Amanda was yelling. "Stop it!"

Something slapped the back of Julia's head. She whirled and saw a flame dancing inches from her face. Instinctively she swatted it away. The torch fell to the ground. Julia saw Amanda's shocked face, saw her reaching for the torch.

Julia snatched it up first, hopped to her feet—and smashed Amanda over the head with it. It was as if an animal had taken control of her body.

An anguished howl pierced the night air.

Julia stood staring, aghast. *I lit her hair on fire!*

She watched as Amanda screamed incomprehensibly—spinning in tight circles like a cat chasing her tail, swiping at the flames creeping down the length of her back.

Without hesitating, Julia threw the torch aside and lunged across the driver's seat, slamming her head against the opposite door. Amazingly, the pain didn't even register. She scrambled to sit up straight as George leaped in beside her. He slammed the door shut.

A peal of thunder shook the air.

"Stop them!" somebody shrieked. "Stop them!"

In the burning chaos a few of the girls rushed forward. George punched the steering column with the base of his fist—once, twice, until a small plastic lid popped open.

Lightning forked through the sky, making the inside of the truck as bright as day. Julia held her breath. George started fumbling with some wires. What was he *doing?* One of the girls reached through the driver's window and grabbed at a clump of George's hair.

"Get offa me!" he shouted.

Bright blue sparks snapped under the steering wheel as another flash of lightning stabbed through the night. A gigantic oak tree about ten feet from the truck burst into flame. The engine roared to life. George stomped his foot—and the truck hurtled forward, throwing Julia's head back.

"Hang on!"

The seat bounced wildly. Julia gazed out the window in horror as bodies and torches tumbled loudly over the hood and fell away . . . they looked like clothing store dummies. She heard screams of anger and pain, the roar of the burning branches, the constant rumbling of thunder.

"Julia!" Luke's voice pierced the air.

"Go!" she yelled. "Just go! Get out of here!"

George flicked on the headlights. The highway swam into view through the narrow corridor of trees. He spun the wheel, skidding onto slick pavement with a loud *screech*. For a few agonizing moments the truck fishtailed . . . then finally, after what seemed like an eternity, it straightened.

It was raining. Huge drops of water pounded on the roof of the car, soaking the windshield.

Julia stared into the darkness, watching the rain fly straight at the window as if it were aimed directly at her. It wouldn't stop now. Somehow she knew the rain wouldn't stop. Maybe not ever.

"We made it," George panted. "We made it!"

Julia nodded. But it was an empty gesture. She

didn't believe him—not even when the liquor store rushed past her window and disappeared into the night.

Now she had proof that the visions were more than crazy, senseless flashes.

Now she had actual *proof* that the visions also jeopardized their lives . . . for some monstrous and unknown reason she didn't understand.

We didn't make it, George, she thought with terrible certainty. *We've only made it for the moment.*

Official Rules
COUNTDOWN
Consumer Sweepstakes

1. No purchase necessary. Enter by mailing the completed Official Entry Form or print out the official entry form from www.SimonSays.com/countdown or write your name, telephone number, address, and the name of the sweepstakes on a 3" x 5" card and mail it to: Simon & Schuster Children's Publishing Division, Marketing Department, Countdown Sweepstakes, 1230 Avenue of the Americas, New York, New York 10020. One entry per person. Sweepstakes begins November 9, 1998. Entries must be received by December 31, 1999. Not responsible for postage due, late, lost, stolen, damaged, incomplete, not delivered, mutilated, illegible, or misdirected entries, or for typographical errors in the entry form or rules. Entries are void if they are in whole or in part illegible, incomplete, or damaged. Enter as often as you wish, but each entry must be mailed separately.

2. All entries become the property of Simon & Schuster and will not be returned.

3. Winners will be selected at random from all eligible entries received in a drawing to be held on or about January 15, 2000. Winner will be notified by mail. Odds of winning depend on the number of eligible entries received.

4. One Grand Prize: $2,000 U.S. Two Second Prizes: $500 U.S. Three Third Prizes: balloons, noise makers, and other party items (approximate retail value $50 U.S.).

5. Sweepstakes is open to legal residents of U.S. and Canada (excluding Quebec). Winner must be 20 years old or younger as of December 31, 1999. Employees and immediate family

members of employees of Simon & Schuster, its parent, subsidiaries, divisions, and related companies and their respective agencies and agents are ineligible. Prizes will be awarded to the winner's parent or legal guardian if under 18.

6. One prize per person or household. Prizes are not transferable and may not be substituted except by sponsors, in event of prize unavailability, in which case a prize of equal or greater value will be awarded. All prizes will be awarded.

7. All expenses on receipt and use of prize, including federal, state, and local taxes, are the sole responsibility of the winners. Winners may be required to execute and return an Affidavit of Eligibility and Release and all other legal documents that the sweepstakes sponsor may require within 15 days of attempted notification or an alternate winner will be selected.

8. By accepting a prize, a winner grants to Simon & Schuster the right to use his/her name and likeness for any advertising, promotional, trade, or any other purpose without further compensation or permission, except where prohibited by law.

9. If the winner is a Canadian resident, then he/she will be required to answer a time-limited arithmetical skill-testing question administered by mail.

10. Simon & Schuster shall have no liability for any injury, loss, or damage of any kind, arising out of participation in this sweepstakes or the acceptance or use of a prize.

11. The winner's first name and home state or province will be posted on www.SimonSaysKids.com or the names of the winners may be obtained by sending a separate, stamped, self-addressed envelope to: Winner's List "Countdown Sweepstakes", Simon & Schuster Children's Marketing Department, 1230 Avenue of the Americas, New York, NY 10020.

Printed in the United States
By Bookmasters